Follow Me, Boys

MacKinlay Kantor

Follow Me, Boys
(God and My Country)

Decorations by
John O'Hara Cosgrave II

GROSSET & DUNLAP

Publishers   New York

To
Murray McMurray

Follow Me, Boys

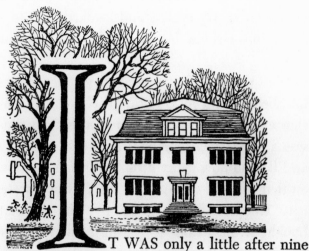

T WAS only a little after nine o'clock in the evening, but already the horde had gone rampaging away. Lemuel Siddons swept them out with jokes and gestures; he said *Scat* and *Scram* by turns, he threatened with pointed finger and clenched fist, he talked of the paper work he must do.

Patrol leaders herded the whole throng into a ring and "America" was screamed duly—just the first verse: that was all they ever sang. Then the cheerleader squatted to his task. Forever the cheerleader was an obstreperous youth with screeching voice, forever his hair hung down over his eyes as he gyrated and pumped his arms.

There had been some twenty-four individuals elected and serving as cheerleaders during the history of the Troop. It seemed to Lem Siddons, as he closed his crusty eyelids and listened, that in some mysterious fashion they had all looked and sounded alike.

"The Drummer" was what they called their tom-tom beater, and by tradition each year he was the shortest boy in any of the four patrols. Sometimes he was a Hawkeye, sometimes a Hound or an Owl or an Elk; and how many drumheads had he worn out on that tomtom since Miss Vida Downey presented it to Troop One, back in 1914? Vida said that she bought it on a railroad platform in Albuquerque, New Mexico, two years before, and carried it gaily all the way home to Iowa, and never imagined just what fine use she would put it to; but in 1914—ah, she knew.

Pink knuckles pounded on taut dirty skin as The Drummer lammed the refrain. Thirty-nine disciplined voices roared the spelling chant in the cadence of a Sioux war dance.

H—I—C—K—O—R—Y!
H—I—C—K—O—R—Y!
H—I—C—K—O—R—Y!
BOY—SCOUTS—A—MER—I—*KY*!

Their last breath went up in a challenging whoop. Old folks or nervous ladies dwelling near the intersection of Elm and Prospect were always holding their ears or making little tchk-tchk sounds with their tongues. Once Grandpa Hedge cried in exasperation when he met Lem on the street, "Siddons, them kids of yours make too blame much noise!"

"Oh, now, Grandpa. Boys have to shout."

"Well, I tell you, you got them kids clean up on the third floor of that schoolhouse, but— I'll be condemned if last night I didn't think they was right in our setting room!"

"After all, Grandpa, it's just for a few minutes, every Friday night."

"Well . . . I 'spose 'tis only once a week. Guess I'll have to make the best of it," and Grandpa Hedge went on his halting way. Then he turned and shook his cane after Lem, and shook his grizzled head under its slouched hat with the stained gold cord. "I'm mighty glad that we never had no Boy Scouts in *my* day."

The voice of a piddling minority, there in the town of Hickory. That was what Lem thought, as he laughed and waved back at Grandpa, and with considerable pride.

So "America," so the yell and hallooing, so the

stamp of nearly eighty feet on the firetrap staircase. Down they went, clattering, blundering, past sacred doors of closed schoolrooms on the second and first floors—the legendary Number Eight and Number Five and Number Three where all the swarm, except those few who had moved to Hickory during recent years, once sat in turn under the tutelage of Miss Smock or Miss Hillock or Miss Shipman.

Always two or three of them hovered long enough to give a few whacks on the gong with which infant classes had been summoned to Turn, Rise and Pass ever since that building went up in 1892. And always Lem would mutter in annoyance, and walk out through a hallway under the ugly mansard roof and call down the echoing stairwell, "Hey, cut that out. That gong's for fire only, and you know it."

Then answering yelps, the slam of heavy doors, silence claiming the Scout hall far above, silence gratefully attentive to Lemuel Siddons' soul.

On this Friday night, however, there arose a quiet scuffle of small footsteps, like the sound of a mouse or bird walking . . . was that a flock of disturbed pigeons tapping on the metal cornices? Lem sat behind the wide kitchen table he used for a desk, and squinted toward the hall shadows.

A small towheaded figure approached from dimness, sheepskin collar turned up and cap in hand.

"Why, Johnny boy. I thought you'd gone with the rest."

"Aw, I thought I ought to come back—" The child wriggled, grinning at Lem. He asked, "Don't you want me to help you with your paper work?"

"Johnny, there's not a thing you can do. Not one solitary blessed thing. I've got two letters to write to National Headquarters and—and— Entries to make in my record ledgers," he added uncertainly. "I'll be here maybe an hour longer. Now, you run home. Your mother knows it was to be an early meeting tonight, and she'd maybe be worried." Lem kept swallowing as he spoke to the boy, but he was smiling still, and winking violently behind his spectacles.

"O.K.," said Johnny agreeably.

"On you," said Lem Siddons, "that brand-new Tenderfoot badge looks pretty good. Yes, sir, *darn* good!"

"Gee, thanks." Eyes were gray-green, gray-green; his face was pale with emotion, but the big eyes glistened with joy.

"Goodnight, Johnny."

"G'night," and the unusual *Sir* which followed the *G'night* floated back from the stairs as if it were spoken by some other lips, shaped by some other mind and heart.

The Scoutmaster sat motionless behind his table until he heard the distant bang of the outer door. Suddenly he had no taste for writing letters, sending in National dues, ordering new Second-Class badges, ordering certificates. There were entries which should be made . . . yes . . . he was tired, in that moment.

No sound but bustling of an animal's busy feet in air-space under the mansard coping. That huge elm tree alongside, and squirrels were bound to use it, to find apertures where they might enter and make their nests. Did squirrels build nests on February 26th? No, of course not . . . or did they? Abruptly Lem felt that he knew nothing about natural history or any other kind of history.

He walked to the west end of the long, alcoved room. Rows of photographs melted beside him as he moved. Snapshots most of them were—some few enlarged—and they clung in rigid masses within wide homemade frames. Campaign hats, faded cotton swimming trunks . . . thin bodies, young bodies,

14

tanned bodies . . . the black inverted V-shape of tent doors . . . boys in front of tents . . . boys, boys, more boys . . . columns in uniform . . . staves, staves: how long since the Scouts had carried staves? Must have given them up about the second year Lem had the Troop. Maybe later. . . .

Lem was not a tall man. He had to stand on tiptoe to look out of the high window which bulged outward from the rusty cornice. Ah, there was Johnny—that dancing dark dot yonder. He had marched in roundabout fashion, skirting bigger puddles in the grass-less schoolyard—regular lakes they were, from the fast melting snow. Snow was nearly gone. Probably they'd have more, however, in March. Even in April. And remember that time when it sleeted on May 12th—

Snow nearly gone, Johnny nearly gone. He was past the old Hedge place; now folks called it the Denaldi house. The late Grandpa Hedge's granddaughter was married to that fellow Denaldi who opened a television repair shop last year. Of course Lem called it the Hedge house, and always would. But—for how long? Well, now, how about it? How long would he be calling anything anything?

Johnny, piece of moving blackness in a browner night, going dutifully past the Waterman house and

15

the O'Fennells'. Then the rainbow-colored fuzz of street light nebula claimed him, swept him to vanishment.

Exactly one thousand and thirty-two voices said unevenly in chorus behind Lem Siddons, and through a room grown spectral: "On my honor, I will do my best to do my duty to God and my country, and to obey the Scout law . . . help other people at all times. . . ." Surely that number of voices, but speaking in miraculous harmony. It was odd that so many voices—some rasping and some smooth and some nasal and some wistful—should be condensed increasingly into the Oath as it was repeated solely by the Johnny who had just walked from sight on the homeward street. All those voices, contained together in Johnny's solitary psalm.

A horse trotted in the wet roadway; Lem heard its hoofs come down. He peered, he couldn't see the horse. Not many horses in Hickory any more, and not nearly so many as there used to be on the farms nearby. Where was that horse?

IT WAS Mayor Hi Plommer's horse, and he progressed up Boone Street, drawing a buggy wherein rode the mayor and the Reverend James G. B. Lesher. It was an icy Sunday afternoon, and young Lemuel Siddons was shoveling fresh-fallen snow as he saw the party approach. He never dreamed that these locally illustrious men were coming to call on him, until they halted by the hitching post.

... Dust the snow from their coats, and bring their overshoes inside, and everybody better put their feet over here toward the register because it's a lot warmer. . . .

Lem kept a big coffeepot on the back of the range, the way his mother always did when she was alive, so he hurried out there and hoped that there was enough coffee left from dinner to do some good. He upset teacups and rattled spoons in embarrassment. It wasn't every day that the mayor and a note-worthy Methodist preacher (who actually wrote editorials for the Des Moines *Capital*, sometimes) came to call on a fellow not yet twenty-four years old.

And Lem was a Congregationalist. He scarcely knew Mayor Plommer, although it was said that his father had known him well. Why did they—?

There was plenty of coffee in the thick seared pot. Which was well, because in another few minutes two more callers arrived, wading through shallow drifts nearby, talking avidly as they came. Father Klepper, the priest, and Professor Barstow, super-intendent of schools.

"Lemuel," said Mayor Plommer, after he had filled his bent-stemmed black pipe and settled it beneath his drooping mustache, "these other gentle-men on this committee have kind of named me as spokesman. Lem, do you know anything about the Boy Scout movement?"

18

. . . Something about England, and a general or something. He had seen a few pictures in magazines. Was it in *McClure's* or *Everybody's*, maybe?

A crying need, declared the Reverend James G. B. Lesher, when the mayor had had his say. No, we feel that it should be something—in this community, at least—divorced entirely from the sponsorship of any single church or sect.

I agree most heartily, said Father Klepper. Those little limbs of— Well, never mind what I was about to say. Some of my altar boys. I think such a movement might reduce the extent of their Confessions!

Laughter, and— Why, thank you, Lem. Yes, I will. Just half a cup.

Apparently it is a proven fact, said Professor Barstow. What few figures are available would indicate that the standard of scholarship has shown gains in those regions where the Boy Scout movement is flourishing. And then—the matter of juvenile delinquency—

But why did you come to me? I'm not very—

Said Mayor Plommer, "Lem, you know my little grandson, Teddy Henderson. Well, his mother was telling me last week how Teddy always hated to buy new clothes. She just had to drag him along, and he'd always make a lot of fuss. But he needed a new

19

suit and long underwear and things, and she said she was going to take Teddy down there to the Mercantile store and get him some duds. And Teddy, he said, 'The Mercantile. Oh, sure, Ma. I should worry—' or something like that. And she wanted to know why, because he always raised such a rumpus before."

The mayor deposited pipe ashes in his coffee saucer. "Good coffee, Lem. Your mother must have taught you how to cook. . . . Well, Teddy he up and says, 'I like to go into the Mercantile.' 'Why?' 'Oh, because I get to talk to Mr. Siddons. He likes all the boys, and he tells interesting stories and stuff, and he knows about pets and Indians and games and things. All the kids like him!' "

The face of Lemuel Siddons was red, amid the general laughter. Additional compliments were offered.

Said Professor Barstow, "I mentioned it to several members of the Board on Friday. That third floor of the south school building isn't used for anything much; it was never completed inside. Just a storage place. I feel confident that if a little money were spent— Maybe some private subscriptions from the businessmen here in Hickory or—"

. . . See, it occurred to us that such a man should

be one who had a certain amount of free time to give to the work. We considered two or three others, but it was agreed to try you first. Of course—uh—you're not married or— And your mother— Was it two years ago that she . . . ?

Little booklets. Here . . . if you'd care to read them over, and give it some thought for a day or so. . . .

Give it some thought for a day or so?

For forty years.

IS FATHER passed away when Lem was five. Then his mother conducted a rooming and boarding house where rooms were always full, where the kitchen was fragrant with sweet odors of baking, with salty smells of browned pot roasts. Thin and clear sounded voices of the schoolteachers who dwelt there; booming rose the ponderous utterance of Judge Margetson, who lived alone and didn't want any nuisance about housekeepers, and came to Mrs. Maudie Siddons for all his meals, even breakfast.

There was a sedate tiger cat named Willis who lived to be thirteen. There was an affectionate mixed-breed collie named Lucy who was always having puppies in closets, on the living room sofa, and once right in the middle of the chaste bed sacred to the slumbers of Miss Cora Senfadder, who had taught mathematics to reluctant minds of young Hickory for nearly two generations.

There was never very much money. Mrs. Siddons had a monthly seesaw battle, trying to keep ahead of her meat and grocery and coal bills. But she owned the solidest bank of peony bushes in that yard, of any yard in town, come June. Red peonies big as cauliflowers, and just about as heavy. Folks used to take walks by there, especially to see those peonies.

Sometimes it seemed to Lemuel, after school and on Saturdays, that the personal barriers which he must assault in life were vegetable mountains—Alps of potatoes to be peeled, whole ranges of green beans to be strung, Canadian Rockies of carrots to be scraped clear and orange.

But there bloomed each year a Christmas tree as tall as a pictured totem pole . . . ah, taffy pulls, when one of the pretty boarders invited her friends into the kitchen on a Saturday night! Lemmy was welcomed along with the grown-up guests, to help haul at jolly ropes of sweetness until they grew pale and ready to be snipped into chunks. Sometimes they put butternuts in the taffy. In after years he could remember how those nutmeats felt, squeezed beneath the pressure of his clean, buttery fingers.

He went down to Ames—that is, to the State College of Agriculture and Mechanic Arts—when he was nineteen, because he had won a scholarship which would help out. Ames was just about the least expensive good college a-going. Lem worked at a restaurant and thus got his meals taken care of; his room didn't cost much. Since he couldn't make up his mind about any particular career (by no means did he feel talented as an agricultural expert or a mechanical engineer) he embraced a liberal arts course, and did very well.

Sometimes he thought that he might really like to teach school. Maybe he should have gone to the State Teachers College at Cedar Falls. But Ames was only nineteen miles from home, and he could walk to Hickory and back, each weekend, if he couldn't catch a ride. Lem dearly loved to take long walks.

He had never been a strapping youth—not much good at football or games like that. But, because he was slim and shy and apt to be picked upon, he absorbed a correspondence school course in boxing and wrestling, and kept a secondhand punching bag out in the empty buggy shed at home.

He'd joined the Iowa National Guards while still in high school, arguing for weeks to win his mother's grudging permission; sometimes they had matches down at the opera house which also did duty as an armory. No one was quite so surprised—and certainly no one quite so delighted—as Lemuel Siddons, when, next summer during the two weeks' camp of the I.N.G.'s, he won the welterweight championship of the Fifty-sixth Iowa. It was gratifying to know that he could take care of himself, and then some.

. . . Hard work, keeping up with his courses at Ames, and waiting table in the restaurant and doing much of the kitchen work too, for such long hours. He insisted that those thirty-eight miles each weekend (often he walked the entire distance) kept him in shape. Though he did lose weight during 1910 and 1911. Then—

A whisper beside him while in botany class, while Doctor Pammel discoursed learnedly on chlorophyll. . . . Siddons. In the Dean's office. It's for you. I don't know: they said it was urgent—

It seemed that there were limits to the hours anyone could spend hovering over a kitchen range. Oh, yes, she used to mention that it did get awfully hot in there, but she didn't really complain.

She lived for two more months speechlessly, unable to move more than the fingers of her left hand. Then she was conveyed to the grassy park on that slope beside a creek; there swelled peony bushes too, though of course not blooming in December. Lem was nearly twenty-two years old, quite alone, reluctant to leave the big shabby house where now only good remembered odors and good remembered songs were boarding and rooming.

There were some accumulated debts, and Lem sold the lots they had owned on Cedar Street, to pay these. He had the house, clear, and taxes wouldn't be more than could be managed in a year's modest savings from a salary.

In Hickory there seemed no appropriate opening for an I.N.G.-summer-camp-welterweight-champion, or for a young man who appreciated especially tales about the Dakotah Nation and the manner in which evening moths approached the Nicotiana flowers (his mother had always called them nick-o-tee-na) during a June dusk. But it was rumored that Mr. Hughes needed someone to take charge of the boys' and young men's ready-to-wear at the Mercantile store, so that was where Lem Siddons went.

. . . Give the sixteen principal points of the compass.

. . . Once again one thousand and thirty-two voices reciting. Yet their blast was simmered into the fragility of a single pale throat and mouth, and the breath of a skinny twelve-year-old with big ears and big gray-green eyes; and maybe his name wasn't Johnny at all: maybe it was Downey.

. . . Volleyed like the spurt of rifles, brought out in a protracted blast, as if those sixteen principal points would be utterly forgotten if they were not announced with explosive haste. *North, north-north-east, northeast, east-northeast, east! East-southeast, southeast, south-southeast, south! South-south-west—*

There were nine boys in the first group to study Tenderfoot tests. They met at Lemuel Siddons' house, sprawled all over the living room, and left the floor carpeted with tag ends of clothesline when they departed. They had been struggling with this business of knot-tying, and what a mess. Well, Lem would learn, and more than knots he would learn.

Next time he made them clean up the whole litter. *A Scout Is Neat.* That wasn't one of the twelve points in the Scout law, but Lem Siddons made it a kind of unofficial thirteenth point.

The Hawkeye patrol was the first one organized, but soon the Troop had enlarged to include fifteen boys, so they founded the Hound patrol. Later came the Elks and Owls. . . . First initiation, and in the new Scout hall for the first time also, on Friday night, February 27th, 1914. There were a lot of parents and aunties and round-eyed little brothers and sisters come to Open Meeting. Every member of the Scout Council lent his presence, not excepting the mayor and Father Klepper. For refreshment Lemuel contributed half a barrel of apples; of course he saw to it that a cleanup committee took care of those cores before everybody went home!

The Reverend James G. B. Lesher intoned a long prayer in closing, and quite by chance someone began to sing "America" under the mistaken impression that it was the official National Anthem. Thus they made "America" part of the ritual, though soon they dispensed with farewell prayers and refreshments. Didn't seem necessary, somehow. The boys were amply satisfied without such things. Cooking food on open fires out by White Fox Creek or Millard's Bridge: that was something else again. That way the Scouts learned the rudiments of cookery; the woods made their own prayer.

O Millard's Bridge the
Troop was bound, one Saturday afternoon in July.
By this time they were twenty-seven strong, and it
was said that other novices were studying up on
tests, hoping to be initiated when a new contingent
was taken in next fall. Twenty-seven noisy varieties
of shouting, to make the welkin ring. (Smiling to
himself, Lem wondered about that: could you call
Millard's Lane a welkin, and how did a welkin really
sound when it rang?)

Striding at the head of the column—proud of his
new khaki uniform with its garish badge, trying to

decide how he should divide the boys for their drill at Morse code with signal flags—this was Mr. Lemuel Siddons, aged twenty-four, in the first moment when he gratified his eyes with the sight of Miss Vida Downey.

She was sitting alone in a black touring car with the top down, on that hill just before you reached the bridge. He remembered, he would remember forever . . . wide-brimmed straw hat with blue ribbons hanging. He would remember the blue-checkered dress, he would remember a brief and wicked and holy glimpse of a tapering ebony silk ankle as he and some Scouts helped her out of the car.

"It's this darn thing," she explained, as the boys clustered around, hoping to be of help. "Can you imagine anything so silly?" Of course they couldn't. Lem knew absolutely nothing about automobiles as yet; he had never owned or driven a car; but some of the Scouts knew. It seemed that when a gearshift lever broke short off above the floor, there was little which could be done, except tow the car to town.

Ah, that broken gearshift lever. It shone like a jewel where the steel had cleanly parted, and the flaw in the steel looked like an embedded diamond. The car was a Jeffreys, said Vida Downey.

(How long since Jeffreyses had been manufactured—or Ramblers or Marions or Velies, or Lexingtons or Moons, or how many others? How long since—Woodrow Wilson? How long since—? Vida Downey in her beauty—?)

Her father was the Mr. John Downey from Marshalltown who had recently purchased the butter and egg depot there in Hickory, from old Mr. Asmundson. More than that: he had bought Mr. Asmundson out—lock, stock and barrel—and Mr. Downey's wife and daughter were now installed and quite at home, thank you, in the Asmundson place on Division Street. Vida had driven down to their farm to get some cherries; here were the cherries, two wide baskets of them, covered with cheese-cloth on the back seat.

Would the Boy Scouts like some cherries?

Ha.

The Troop clamored for the privilege of visiting the nearest farm and telephoning Parkhurst's garage, so that the Jeffreys could be hauled to town. A stone-throwing contest was held promptly, and two winners went posting away, well provisioned with fat red cherries. The rest of the Troop, and the Scoutmaster, kept Vida Downey company. They relaxed in shade on the slope above the road, after they had pushed the disabled touring car to one side.

Oh, far away a distant thrilling, a bubbling fairy sound. . . .

"I'm trying to learn the birds," said Lem. "I mean —we're all trying. But that one's got us licked. Do you know it?"

"Which sound?" she asked.

"Way over there in the woods. Wait a minute; maybe it'll sing again."

She sat with lips half parted in the unconscious attitude of listening, and a light warm wind came twitching; loose strands of filmy red-brown hair lifted from her neck, and then settled cosily back again.

"There—" and for a wonder the whole Troop was silent.

"Why, of course," cried Vida Downey. "The least flycatcher!" Sure enough, it was.

. . . Many small humorous freckles—lighter on her cheeks and wrists, but spattered like specks of bright paint on her tilted nose. The boys trotted back from the Stevens' house and said that men were coming soon from Hickory, to tow the car.

One band of Scouts was sent down the river through the timberland with instructions to make a trail; the other half must wait ten minutes exactly,

then try to trail the first pack, and catch them before
they returned safely to Home Base by a circuitous
route. This was a new stunt they'd never tried before; the idea came like light from heaven to Lem
Siddons; he was ecstatic because he had dreamed it
up. The boys took quite a while about the whole
enterprise, and the men from Parkhurst's had a flat
tire on the way.

"I hear your Boy Scouts in the woods, Mr. Siddons."

"My name is Lemuel. Lem for short. What's yours,
did you say? Ida?"

"No, it's Vida. Oh, listen to them yelling! That
other bunch must have caught up with them.
They're just making the welkin ring!"

"Now, that's a point, Vida Downey. I've been
wondering about that."

"What—uh—Lem?"

"Just what is a welkin, and how does it ring?"

"Don't be silly. Why, it's—maybe a little valley?"

"Are you sure?"

"Well—no."

"Maybe it's something like freckles. Equally
beautiful, spread all over everywhere—"

"Honestly, you've got a lot of nerve!"

"Did you say—Congregational?"

"Mother and I were at church last Sunday, for the first time. We didn't see *you*."

"Goodness' sake, I haven't been in a coon's age. But seemed to me I heard something about a supper in the church basement on Wednesday night—"

"Yes, they put Mother and me on the committee so fast it would make your head swim, after we told Reverend Metcalf we'd be joining by letter."

"What are they going to have to eat?"

"Chicken pie, peas, parsley potatoes—"

"Stop. You're killing me! We won't be cooking supper for hours. . . . Well, I see I've got to get my religious life in hand. Do you think that Reverend Metcalf will be preaching about the Pilgrims again tomorrow? He usually preaches about them."

"He did last Sunday, most certainly."

"I'm crazy about Pilgrims! And in this work, as Scoutmaster, I think I ought to know more about Pilgrims than I do! Also about least flycatchers. Also about freckles—"

"Golly, but you Hickory fellows are *fresh*."

"Not all of them. Just me."

"Isn't that a car coming? Oh, it must be the men from the garage! I hope they brought a good strong tow-rope. And *here* comes your Scout Troop—"

"Yeh, doggone it."

They helped with the rope, as much as the garage men would let them; they helped with this and that; they took their final ration of cherries. Vida sat up behind the wheel; the men cautioned her about braking carefully on the creek hill, coming into town.

Goodbye, goodbye. Goodbye, Boy Scouts! Goodbye—ah—Mr. Scoutmaster.

Goodbye. The two cars started jerking away up the incline, then settled into a steady pull and an easy following. *Goodbye, Miss Vida Downey. Hey, there, Troop—how about giving Miss Downey our yell?*

H-I-C-K-O-R-Y—

Floppy straw hat, and a turn and waving, and blue ribbons in the sun, blue ribbons in the sun forever, the sun shining forever.

At the head of his Troop, Lem Siddons marched the riverbank. Signal flags would be unfurled one hour and twenty-nine minutes later than he had planned to unfurl them. Lem's soul sang a more winning song than any least flycatcher, any delicate woodsy bundle of feathers and melody which the good Lord ever made.

AYOR PLOMMER
came into the back room at the Mercantile and sat
down on the table where Lem was unpacking a ship-
ment of celluloid collars. "Lem, do you know that
kid Kermit—or Kermie—Joyce?"

Lem did. "Oh, yes—that little tad. The kids call
him 'Creamy.' What's the trouble?"

Plenty of trouble, it seemed. There'd been com-
plaints about a back window broken out or a door
lock fiddled with, here and there: a kind of petty
thievery which was more guessed at than observed.
But the door of Pappas's candy store was given

special scrutiny by the old night watchman, so there had accumulated a peck of trouble about three o'clock that morning.

The watchman nabbed the Joyce kid. His pockets and the bag of his dirty blouse were stuffed full of candy and chewing gum.

"Not much, as money goes," said the mayor, "but still it's Breaking and Entering. He hadn't tried to fool with the cash register, either. Couldn't get a word out of him—why he did it, and was he going to sell the candy, or anything like that. The watchman brought him up to my house, and I talked to him like a Dutch uncle. He cried, a little, but still he wouldn't talk."

Lem was very unhappy. He was always unhappy, and had a feeling of worthlessness and utter futility, whenever he heard of a kid getting mixed up in something like this. "Did you tell his folks?"

"Had to. Guess his mother was—you know—she's usually running around with a fast crowd over in Fort Dodge or somewhere. Travelling men and such. But his father came and took him home, and I 'spose he beat the daylights out of him."

"Probably he did, if he was drunk as usual," said Lem bitterly. "Ed Joyce is about the best master plumber we ever had in this town, if he'd only stay sober. But he's shiftless and doesn't half feed his family." He lowered his voice. "Mr. Hughes had him here at the store; supposed to install some new equipment in the washroom; that was last month. Drunk for days on end—pipes lying all over this back room—and in the end we had to get another plumber."

. . . They lived in a shady series of dark rooms over a broken-down grocery store, in a side street filled mainly with implement shops and feed stores. The two older boys had run away—to the Navy, it was said. Kermit Joyce was slight and round-shouldered and bore a perpetual frown between his grayish brows. His hair was the color of grayish sand, too; his face looked like that of a little old man, beaten and squeezed.

Other children gave him a wide berth. He could fight like a fiend—and did, nearly every day. It was alleged that he had given a black eye to that gangling sixteen-year-old kitchen boy at the Imperial Hotel.

" 'Tain't really his fault, but he's a little hellion for sure," sighed the mayor. "Looks like he'll land down at Eldora before you can say Jack Robinson . . . flinks school every week, and then the marshal has to go hunting him. Usually he's in the alleys somewhere. I've never heard anything good about him."

Lem thought about it. "I have," he said. "At least I saw something very good."

"What was that?"

Lem Siddons told him, and the mayor lifted bushy eyebrows. A dog had been hurt, over in the railroad yards somewhere, and it crawled into a packing case behind Katz & Oppenheim's store. Apparently Creamy Joyce found the dog there. Several times Lem saw him sneaking furtively up the alley with a bucket of water or a pan which seemed to contain food.

"Hyman Katz finally discovered the dog—dead— in that packing box," Lem concluded. "But someone had made a little bed for it out of rags and excelsior, and if that someone wasn't Creamy Joyce, then I don't know who it was."

"Now, what do you know about that!"

"I wish he were older. I'd try to get him in the Scouts. Might do him some good."

"Why, how old do you think he is?"

"Oh, ten or eleven—"

"Well, he's not. He's thirteen years old, or so his father told me. Just small for his age."

"Malnutrition, probably."

"Maybe so, maybe so."

Lem slapped the table, and all the celluloid collars

danced and rolled. "Mayor, let me work on this a little," and so the mayor let him.

His plot included a bottle of blood-colored India ink, and the services of Pansy, the store cat. Since she had a family creeping amid crushed tissue paper in an old crate, Pansy could be trusted to remain readily available, purring amiably close at hand.

Two or three times Lem saw that unhappy soiled shape scooting down the alley, hurling steel bolts at glass insulators on the electric light poles—bolts stolen from the junkyard, probably. But there were always customers to be waited on, or Mr. Hughes was nearby, or one of the girl clerks.

Then, during the noon hour next Tuesday, no customer was in the store and neither was Mr. Hughes. Creamy Joyce came by, and Lem dove for the astonished Pansy.

He dabbed a front paw generously with ink, and caught up the clean white rags he'd prepared in advance. Out on the loading platform . . . "Hey, there, boy!"

Creamy turned and gave him the expression of an angry monkey.

"Wonder if you'd come and help me? This cat has got her foot hurt."

Creamy came.

. . . Lem explained, "This is the way you put a foot bandage on a cat or a dog. But it's a lot easier if you have two or more to do it. . . . That's right. Thanks. Hold her that way and she can't scratch you—much. Poor kitty. . . ."

Creamy said nothing, but Lem threw a quick glance over his shoulder when he went questing for more bandages, and saw a dirty brown hand gliding lightly over the cat's gray fur.

"She's got some kittens in that box."

"Where?"

"Over under that bench. . . Yes, we do a lot of this sort of work, with animals, in the Boy Scouts."

The hard brown eyes sneered up at him. "Boy Scouts are a bunch of sissies! Think they're smart, going around, trying to play soldier. I could lick any of them."

"Oh, could you? Don't try to take on Kenneth Neel or Brad Mason or Bill Cessna or—"

"Well, I could!"

Pansy was now fully done up in white muslin and splints. She went hobbling resentfully into her box, where she set to work ripping at the bandage. Lem let a torn envelope fall from his pocket, and the contents spilled on the floor. "Doggone it. Here, help me pick these up, will you, before they get dirty?"

"What's all those little pieces of cloth?" growled Creamy.

"Just some merit badges. For the Scouts."

"Do they get to wear that stuff?"

"Only if they qualify by passing a lot of tests. Believe me, some of those tests are pretty stiff. These are the first badges like this which anyone has won in the Troop. Of course, we only started last winter—"

"What's this red-and-green one, with the cross?"

"First Aid. . . . See, this is Personal Health—this one with the heart on it. Well, well," and he chuckled easily, and put the next badge into Kermit Joyce's ready hand, for him to examine. "What a coincidence! That's First Aid to Animals. Of course, to win that badge a guy would have to do a lot more than help bandage a pussycat," he added, scornfully.

Kermit mumbled something, and received Lem's warm thanks, and went on his way. But he was back again, suddenly, fifteen minutes later, like a thin gnome projected suddenly across the loading platform in one bounce.

"Say. How much does it cost to join the Boy Scouts?" Again that single volley of breath—

Southwest, west-southwest, west! West-northwest, northwest—

"Not exactly a million dollars. Naturally, you have to pass some tests. There's a very small initiation fee, and then some annual dues—"

"Do you have to fight anybody?" asked Creamy with hope.

"Not unless you start something first. By the way, I hear you're pretty handy with your dukes. You know, I used to box, myself. Welterweight—"

"Were you good?"

"Well, I did get a little cup or two."

"Have you got 'em here at the store?"

"No, they're out home. Sometime I'll show you. . . . By the way, my yard's in terrible shape: box-elder leaves all over it. Most of the fellows I know have got part-time jobs, or work at home. I wonder if you might know some kid who would be willing to do some yard work—say, twenty cents an hour—"

Pansy made a triumphant leap from the crate, free of her bandage. Though still her fur was colored, she walked without a limp, and Creamy Joyce thought that this was a miraculous cure.

EAVES HAD been
painted brightly in most other autumns of Lemuel's
life. Now they were not only painted—they were
drenched, they were a garden, a galaxy, a battle-
field, an orchard. They were God and all saints and
apostles and alabaster and carmine (in his secret
murmurings Lem called it *Carmen*, and would
eternally) and lemon . . . oh gold, oh burnt pink
husk, oh enchanted wand and paintbrush, oh tints
upon a fabled Pottawatomie medicine bag when the
dusk came fiery. . . .

They called it North Hills; in time the region

would be subdivided, but not until the town grew—not yet, not yet. Marching above riverside cottonwoods and willows the hills went bristling along, and some of them still wore their native prairie grass; therefore pasque flowers were purplish cotton there each spring, and bees fed thick.

Therefore the summits which had given birth to a few oaks and reared them well—these summits had their own dye and their own paradise. Hazel brush wallowed scraggly away to the north behind, and there were lone walnut trees where the pungent balls were beaten down in any even-numbered year, and groves of hardy butternuts to feed upon in odd-numbered years. (Some people thought that was a myth, but Lem had learned that it worked out that way.) There were arrowheads to be picked up, and crows to squawl at you, and the smoke of town to be observed, and usually a bull to be watched out for.

Vida had a fuzzy-gray sweater and a tam to match. This was late on a Sunday afternoon, so the only lunch brought along was a batch of ginger cookies in Vida's pocket. They were due to have prosy tea and sliced-meat-loaf sandwiches with Mr. and Mrs. Downey when evening came . . . evening was far, far; the sun hung smoky.

"Lem, you're very good."

"What say, lady?"

"That boy. Kermit Joyce. The whole story comes out between the lines. And— Well, Mrs. Mayor Plommer told my mother—"

"Heck, I haven't done much. He's got a long row to hoe, poor kid. Oh, Vida, I forgot to tell you: we had election Friday night, and Creamy was made Drummer. 'Course, that's because he's the smallest, but I guess it will help."

"Everything will help, Lem. So will you. You help them all."

They sat in thick-fallen leaves, they bent close and dangerously intimate, they were very near to lying together among the wild crisp powders.

"Heck, I'm just trying to—"

"Tell me. What are you trying to do?"

"It's just that— The boys— Well, I get a lot out of them, too."

She sat up and stared at him. "You must. I think you're the richest young man I ever met. Take that Chinese boy—what's his name? Quong Lee?—from the laundry. He thought the other boys wouldn't want him, but you talked him into it; and now you say he's just about the most popular kid in the Troop and won all those races and things."

"Lee's making a swell Scout. He—"

"And what about Pinkie MacPhee? He wasn't going to join, because he has to wear braces on both legs; and last spring he threw stones at the boys when they marched past his house; but you said he made a new record for transition from Tenderfoot to Second Class. Lem, can't you see how good you are? You're helping to make *lives*."

His arms were around her, and they were kissing in their nest of leaves, and her smell was one new wonder amid the mingled autumn scents. He was kissing with a fury and a dedication, as he had never kissed any other girl. For a moment it seemed that she responded. Then—

"Lem, let me up." Muffled.

"No, I won't. Vida, this is it! This is what I want—"

"No, no! *Lem!* Someone might see—"

"Isn't anybody. We're clear out here—"

"*Lem!*" Her struggle was so intense that it could not be ignored, could not be overridden or restrained. He sat up and let her sit, twisting away from him and breathing heavily.

He muttered, "Vida, here's what I've been trying to say, and you said it for me. That's it—that's what I want to do. Make lives. With you—that's who I want to make them with. I want to marry you and live with you, and love you, and have kids. I guess if we did our part, God would do the rest! Vida, darling, please look at me. I—I love—"

She said slowly, face still averted, "No, Lemmy. Thank you. You—you're very sweet—as well as good. But I can't marry you. It's impossible."

"I thought maybe you—"

"No. You're wrong. I do thank you, darling Lem, but it's quite—out of the question." And now strangely Vida was gasping in a new manner, and her voice sounded like a stranger's.

Lem sat stricken, watching the town smoke lazy in the pale blue sky, the low sun beginning to make brass of that smoke. He heard crows; they were mournful and far away.

"Vida. Is it because I'm just—? Look here, I'm still pretty young, as businessmen go in these parts. I'm not making much of a salary, but I won't be clerking in drygoods all my life. I do own a house— 'course, I inherited it, but—"

She said evenly, "Lem Siddons, if you keep talking like that I'll never speak to you again! Of course that's not it. I'm not thinking about—money, and a big salary. How dare you?"

Then louder, and more and more hysterically, she kept crying. *How dare you?* and actually she was striking him with her hands. In one more moment he had never heard a woman sob as she was sobbing.

"Vida! Angel— I didn't mean— What on earth . . . ?"

Somehow she made human tones at last, or inhuman tones, a muffled snarl and tragedy. "It's— I was in a runaway when I was thirteen; I never told you. And they—the doctors said— In Marshalltown and—and the one in Chicago where my folks took me— They said they—didn't think—I could ever have any children. Oh, Lem, not *ever!*"

Vida Marie Downey and John Lemuel Siddons were married at the home of the bride, on Saturday, December 19th, 1914. This came about after an October evening discussion between Lem and John Downey, in which Mr. Downey made so bold as to hint that Lem was maybe looking for— Well, Mr. Downey knew that he himself was pretty well off, and he kept a mighty sharp eye on all the young whippersnappers who came hanging around Vida, and— Well, if Lem had a little more of a—what you might call a competence, why—

Lem showed as much temper on that night as he would need to demonstrate to anyone in the next generation of his life. The result was a chastened if grumpy Mr. Downey, a weeping Mrs. Downey, a beaming daughter, and a mildly intoxicated Lem.

49

Probably he was the first man in history to become drunk on hot chocolate.

Troop One, Boy Scouts of America, attended the afternoon wedding at the insistence of the bride and mingled socially with scads of Marshalltown guests. The quantity of creamed turkey, fruit salad, bread-and-butter sandwiches, and grape juice dispensed became one of those hoary old wives' tales whispered through the ages by grandmothers at their firesides.

John Downey Siddons, to be called Downey, was born on December the 8th, 1916, by Caesarean section. By the time he began to assume a more-or-less palatable appearance, it was observed that he had enormous ears and a calm and tender gaze, like his father. His eyes became a dulcet green-gray or gray-green, the exact color of Vida's old sweater.

IN THIS manner Vida's parent was made both grandfather and godfather in one swoop. Of course Lem's first name was John, too; always he had loathed the name Lemuel, but wore it philosophically out of respect to a grave man he could barely remember.

Vida had to rest in the hospital for several weeks after the birth of her son. But Scout activities must proceed as usual; Lem had his obligation. He came racing back from the hospital on the evening of the 29th, to unlock the hall and scurry through last-minute chores concerning the annual holiday party.

It was given during the week between Christmas and New Year's, and each Scout had the right to invite a non-Scout friend.

"I'm so amused at Dad," Vida had said, when Lem sat beside her bed, feeding her poached eggs. "You'd think the baby was his! He drives up here three and four times a day, and hovers, and makes silly little noises when he thinks no one is listening to him. He's already planning how he's going to teach Downey to candle eggs, after school hours!"

Lem's laugh was a bit mechanical.

She looked at Lem earnestly. "Please don't be hurt or annoyed. Downey is your child, not Daddy's, and he doesn't have to candle a single egg if you don't want him to. But let Dad have fun for the time being. He always wanted a boy and only got—me."

For that reason Lem was not perplexed—only slightly surprised—when the big brown-clad figure of John Downey blocked the door that night just as yammering Scouts and guests were being divided into teams for the charades and innocent duels. Mr. Downey received many curious stares; for a moment there was a lull. Lem welcomed the new guest and showed him to a rear bench, where he bulked motionless and observing.

Not in those two years had he ever attended an Open Meeting, nor was this an Open Meeting now.

He explained, when Lem could come to sit with him briefly, "Just thought I'd like to see what kind of an organization my grandson is going to be tangled up with."

Lem was inspired to place John Downey as a minor performer on one team and himself as a minor performer on the other. The guest showed an unexpected talent at roughhouse charades; beet-faced and lumbering he fought a game but losing battle during the potato race; seriously he mimicked the antics of Patrol Leader Pinkie MacPhee in rubbing his finger on the bottom of a plate and making the identical motions against his face which Pinkie made. Since Pinkie's plate was clean, and the bottom of Mr. Downey's plate was anointed with candle-wick-soot, the results put the boys in stitches, and sent the baffled Mr. Downey downstairs to the washroom.

He lingered after "America" and the yell and tomtom, he lingered after the party had broken up, and helped Lem to pack baskets. He walked across the schoolyard with him.

"I thought it was more military than this."

"Well, of course the Scouts didn't wear their uniforms because it was a party, not a regular meeting. But we don't stress the military at all."

"But it's not a religious thing, either?"

"Definitely not. This country's always had plenty of Sunday School classes, but they couldn't fill the same function that the Scouts fill."

"Why all this stuff about the woods—animals and birds and—? Look at it practically, Lem. Most of these kids aren't going to be living in the woods after they grow up. They're going to be living in towns."

"Stop," said Lem, and the amazed Downey obeyed him, there amid stiff dark snowbanks of Prospect Street. "It's pretty cold tonight. Suppose you were walking on the river ice, for one reason or another, and the ice gave way, and you fell in. What would you do?"

"I'd streak right off for home," Mr. Downey declared in his best common-sense tone.

"Not if you were a well-taught Scout, you wouldn't! That's courting pneumonia, freezing to death—any such disaster. No, you'd build a fire, and then you'd make two fires out of it, and you'd stand between them until you dried yourself. *Then* streak for home."

"But my matches would be all wet."

54

"You'd have waterproof matches in your pocket."

"How would that be? I never carried any in my life."

"But you aren't a Scout. One of the first things my boys are taught about winter hiking is never to travel over snow and ice without carrying some waterproof matches. The boys make their own."

"How?"

"This way—"

Ordinarily they would have separated, there on Prospect, but this night Mr. Downey accompanied Lem all the way out to the Boone Street house, and had two cups of coffee before he went home. Inspired by the thought of his own tiny son, inspired by recollection of the ninety-odd young spirits amidst whom they had been mingling that night, Lem was articulate as he opened his heart to this man he'd considered to be a thick-headed and somewhat grasping individual, even if he was Vida's father.

"I get it," said Downey, "and I think you're right. Boys like to go in the woods anyway—I used to, years ago, down there in Marshall County—and you're correct when you say that the woods are the world's best classroom!"

Lem brandished the coffeepot. "If a boy can gain

self-assurance and self-respect in the woods, he's not going to lose that self-respect and that ability, no matter where he goes!"

"Lem, I think it's going to be a fine thing for Downey, when his time comes. Think he'll make a good Scout?"

"He's got every earmark," cried Lem Siddons, twitching his own big ears which he had awarded to that pint-sized creature at the hospital. He and his father-in-law parted jovially and in mutual appreciation.

He liked to think of that night. They never had another one like it. Downey the Son was just getting over his colic, and the exhausted Vida was sleeping beside the baby's crib during a spring afternoon, and the exhausted Lem was selling nightshirts to none other than Mayor Hi Plommer, when he was called to the telephone. The mayor had his new car parked in front of the Mercantile. In another moment he and Lem were flying toward the butter and egg depot on Osage Street.

They could have taken all the time they pleased. John Downey was lying on the couch behind his desk—clerks had lifted him from the floor—and Dr. Desmond was putting away his stethoscope. "Quick is good," said the doctor, thinking of a miserable patient whose bed he had deserted to rush here. "But it's too bad. He was only about fifty-four, wasn't he, Lem?"

AID Ed Joyce, drunker than any skunk or lord, "I been meaning to—talk to you. Bout my kid Kermit. You—you just bout made a sissy out of him. I seen him go out of his way to avoid a scrap—yes, I did! Y-yesterday. That big Haskins kid . . . I would of give Kermie a good belting if I'd of caught him. But—it's your fault. And them damn Scouts—yes, it is!"

Lem told him, "Be quiet, Ed. Kermit's doing fine. He's got a good job at the drug store, after school and Saturdays, and they swear by him—not at him."

"I don't want my son to be no sissy!"

58

"He'll never be. As for that sloppy fat Tod Haskins, he can't fight for shucks. Just makes a lot a bluster. Creamy didn't want to hurt him, that's all."

"Well—"

"Ed, why'n't you go home and go to sleep for awhile?"

"Well—"

"Come on, I'll walk down there with you. Come on, before the marshal sees you. Here, lean on my shoulder. Come on, let's go."

"Well—"

Ed walked in front of Willson & Brady's big moving van, just eight days later, but living or dead he could have had very little further effect on Kermit Joyce. Creamy was the first Eagle Scout in the history of Troop One, at the age of fifteen.

. . . Said Pedro Corral, "I wait to see you, Mr. Siddons. I no like for Luis to be Boy Scouts."

"Why not, Pete? Why on earth—?"

"Because Boy Scouts, they make them to be soldiers, shoot down poor workingman. I know. I poor Mexican, I work for railroad, but one time I work in California before I come here. Soldiers, they come with guns when we go on strike! Boy Scouts—I know! They got same what you call it—uniform—"

"Pete, you're Luis's father, and it's your right to

say whether or not he should be a Scout. But will you do me one favor?"

"I—I no—"

"Promise me you'll come with Luis to the Open Meeting next Friday. Then, after you've seen what we do and how we do it, you can let Luis be a Scout or not, just as you choose."

"I no got good clothes! See, all I got—overalls! Our house burn down last spring— All I got—"

"If I wear overalls too, will you come, with Luis?"

"O.K. I come."

. . . Said Mr. J. Owen Bunker, "Why, hello, Lem. I wondered who was knocking at our door this dark and stormy night, ha, ha! Come in, come in. . . . Yes, he's been in bed quite awhile. . . . Alone? Why, of course. Honey, would you mind . . . ?"

"This is rather important, Bunk."

"Why, Lem, I— Go ahead, we can talk in here. What's on your mind, anyway?"

"Bunk, you know damn well what's on my mind. Jackie gave me his name as a prospective Scout, and said he was studying his tests. Then all the other kids showed up except Jackie. Sometimes boys' gossip is not very accurate, sometimes it is. Did you tell Jackie you didn't want him to join the Scouts?"

"Well, I— Yes. It was on account of his mother. She raised Cain, Lem—literally raised Cain!"

"Why?"

"Oh, it's on account of her brother's boys, in Chicago. They joined the Scouts there, a year or so ago. Went to camp in the summer, down along the sand dunes somewhere— Lem, it's a pretty nasty business. I hate to talk about it."

"I hate to come here on such an errand. Go ahead."

"Well, there was this Scoutmaster—always prominent in boys' work at churches and so on—and he— Well, it wasn't only my nephews that had the experience, either! Some of the others reported the same thing. One night, this Scoutmaster, he—"

Haltingly he told about the occurrence.

"Bunk, what happened to the Scoutmaster?"

"He got kicked out, of course. Maybe he got put in jail, too, for all I know. But, you see, when Carrie heard about it, it left a pretty bad taste in her mouth. She just didn't like the idea of Boy Scouts any more, and so she insisted that Jackie—"

"Do you think I'm that kind of man?"

"Godsakes, no, Lem! Why, you're a pillar of the community and—"

"Never mind about my being a pillar of anything. Bunk, do you sell good Early Ohio potatoes at your store?"

"Why, what's that got to do with—? Sure. Best in town."

"Maybe so. I bought a bushel last week, and found two big rotten ones in the bottom—all gooey, all worm-eaten and squashy—"

"I'm sorry. Why didn't you tell me?"

"It was an accident. You handle a lot of potatoes, and so it was entirely possible that a few bad ones might have gotten by you."

"Ha, ha. I see what you're driving at. Pretty clever—"

"Not especially; it's just an honest statement of a fact. I threw out the bad potatoes, and made sure that the ones right next to them hadn't been infected. But I didn't say that all Early Ohio potatoes stunk. I didn't say, 'I'll never buy a thing at Bunker's grocery store again.' I figured it was an accident. And Vida has cooked a lot of those other good potatoes, and they tasted swell!"

"Lem, you kind of make me ashamed of myself."

"Good. Will you talk to—?"

"Carrie? You're darn tooting I will. Tonight!"

. . . Said young Professor Henry Olpe, high school

science teacher, "I have a plan which would be good for your Boy Scouts."

"Swell. Go ahead and shoot, Professor."

"What—? *Ja.* I talk to you about the marching of the boys. I see them in the parade on—on Decoration Day, before I go away for the summer. They march bad. I regret I should say this to you, but they are so—so sloppy. Young boys should not march so!"

"How should they march?"

"Proud they should march! Quick—what you call —smart! Like this: *one, two— One, two!* It is so in Germany when the young boys march. Not any of your boys, do they keep in step! I was considering to help you. The correct marching I have been taught, long ago, but I have not forgotten. Now, each week I come to you and your Boy Scouts— I give my own time for the good of this town—*ja.* Your boys you will call together, and I teach them. Maybe they have some little wooden guns, *nein*? I teach—"

"Excuse me, Professor. That's very kind of you, and I do appreciate your offer. But we are not a— well, a marching-out kind of organization. To me, to the boys, to the whole world, it doesn't matter in the least because the boys are not in step. This is a free-and-easy kind of world, here in America; and if the

Scouts march kind of free-and-easy—I think it's all to the good."

"But in Germany it would—"

"We're not living in Germany, thank God. Professor, why did you come to America?"

"I come because I like my studies, my work, my science of nature best of all. But that does not mean—"

"Did you serve in the Army, over there?"

"I was trained. But in the real Army I did not go—"

"Isn't it a fact that you came over here to avoid military service under the Kaiser? Didn't you really run away to America to escape just that?"

"*Nein*, I did not run! I come—"

"Look, you could really do something for us that would help a lot. Some of the boys are getting interested in collecting butterflies and beetles and spiders and critters like that. I don't know too much about such things, and I'd like to know too. Now, how about coming over and giving us a little lecture, at regular Scout meeting—you know, about fifteen minutes—just enough to sink in, not too much all at once. Maybe two or three meetings, in a row? How to collect specimens, preserve them, fix them up in a collection—how to identify the various kinds— A lot of the kids won't be in your science classes for several years yet."

"*Ja, ja, ja!* That is good. I come! I bring some specimens. I show—"

. . . Again Dr. Desmond put away his stethoscope, but this time there was no motionless figure lying on a couch nearby; only Lemuel Siddons, stripped to his waist and standing pathetically in the middle of the doctor's private office.

"What's the verdict, Doc?"

"Hickory!" said the doctor shortly.

It took a minute or so for Lem to receive the full impact. "You mean—that I couldn't get by? The Army doctors—?"

"Lem, what year did you leave the I.N.G.'s?"

"When my militia enlistment ran out. But what—?"

"Well, I consider that a decision by the Almighty! Now, an Army surgeon might or might not pass you. It's the old ticker, Lem. You can't be very certain about these things. One man says Yea, another Nay. It's a kind of borderline case. Did you ever submit your heart to a severe strain, when you were a kid?"

Lem thought about it. "If you could call walking here and back, from Ames, the way I did when I was in college—"

"Emphatically yes. I remember seeing you do it. You used to be practically running when you came into town and when you left. That could have done it. Something did. I'd say you had a real athlete's heart. You might live to be ninety. On the other hand, a moderately severe wound or illness could finish you off—quick—like poor John Downey."

Suddenly the import was more than Lem could bear. He sat down in Doctor Desmond's chair, and cradled his head on his folded arms. "I wish I could go to France," came the muffled voice.

"Sure." The doctor grinned under his rough mustache and came over and snapped Lem's bare neck with his thumb. "So do a lot of us. Fat chance I've got, with all my kids. Lem, what would happen to the Scouts, if you went?"

"I suppose—somebody else—"

"Just who?"

"I don't know."

"I do hate slushy songs," said Dr. Desmond, "but there's such a thing as Keeping the Home Fires Burning. Lem, tell me honestly—as your doctor, and

I hope you believe you can trust me—were you trying to run away from anything?"

Wheels rumbled in the main street for a time, and downstairs in the drugstore a phonograph kept grinding out, *You're like a sweetheart of mine. From ocean to ocean, for you my devotion. . . .*

Lem said, "Well, Vida and her mother— You know, with Mr. Downey's death— He left the entire property to Mrs. Downey; so she and Vida want me to leave the Mercantile store and go down and take over the butter and egg depot. Manage the business, run it on shares—"

"Why don't you do it? You'd make more money than you're making; you'd have more leisure; you'd have more time for the Scouts."

"Yes, but I don't know anything about butter and eggs."

"You didn't know anything about men's and boys' ready-to-wear when you went to the Mercantile, either. Mr. Hughes taught you. Those employees down there in the business—first with Asmundson, then with Downey—they can teach you. Ellingson, Mathre—all the rest. Old Miss Currie and young Beale. You'll be among friends."

The doctor sat beside Lem and said, "Two dollars

for the examination, ten thousand dollars for the advice, and cheap at that. Lem, don't let your family down and don't let the Scouts down. We need you here in Hickory, more than ever, with a war going on. If you could manage to get into the service—which I strongly doubt—you'd have no guarantee of getting overseas. You're more valuable to the Nation and to the community—right here, doing exactly what you've been doing with our kids—than you'd be sitting in a little tent down in Horned Toad, Texas!"

After a time the doctor said, "Right?"

Lem muttered, "Call me a butter and egg man." Sulkily he began to put on his shirt, but he couldn't help responding to the doctor's grin. "Tell that Thomas of yours that he's still got to finish building a bridge across Lyons Creek before he can get his merit badge for Pioneering!"

Land where my faaathers died,
Land of THY Pilgrums pride,
From eh-eh-ehvry mountun side. . . .

ONE thousand and thirty-two voices, according to smudged listings in the ledgers, and it was odd that they sang so softly. For that was really a pretty big chorus, bigger than anyone else in the town of Hickory had ever listened to or ever would listen to.

Lem Siddons had heard something about a Vatican choir. He wondered vaguely how many boys' voices were in it.

Two service flags in that room . . . the flag from World War One hung high over the east window alcove. Ugly glaring electric lamps, fastened upon the ceiling, gave no light to that flag. They cast it in shadow, and so did the dust. Lem felt guilty, considering dust. Just when had he last taken down that flag and shaken it? Next week he'd better have some of the kids get a stepladder and crawl up there and unfasten the flag and—

Ordinarily there was enough heat left in the pipes to last through an evening session, but this was well past the hour for termination of any nighttime activity in the hall. Lem found himself shivering. He draped his overcoat around his shoulders, but still he didn't want to go home. The elder service flag was a magnet of cobwebby bunting which drew him down the room.

Sixteen blue stars, three gold ones. The gold had turned to a coppery brown. Those stars signified two boys who had died in the S.A.T.C. during the Flu epidemic, and one who had been awarded the Distinguished Service Cross. Posthumously.

> Quong, Corp. Lee T. (Deceased). For Extraordinary Heroism in action at Durronches, France, on September 29th, 1918. When enemy machine guns halted the ad-

vance of his company, Corp. Quong
equipped himself with a bag of hand gre-
nades and, although already wounded, ad-
vanced alone under heavy fire to a point
where—

So long ago, so long ago. Old Quong Sam, Lee's
father, together with the elderly uncle or great-
uncle or cousin or whatever he was, had sold out
their little laundry and gone back to China after the
war. A chain grocery bustled now on the site of that
narrow tin-sided building. Two modern laundries
in town today and a drive-in laundromat as well.
Lem wondered what Lee would think of these in-
truders, if he could see. Doubtless his tiny eyes
would disappear in a leering smile, as they used to
do, and he would say nothing.

Quong Lee had been a natural-born patrol leader
and Lem's son Downey had been another. Years
later, naturally . . . Downey was still staggering on
his feet, still talking in grunts, when Lee vanished
in the Argonne.

Lem Siddons stood in the chill, blinking back the
tears. Golly, Vida had been difficult at times . . . he
supposed all women were.

"I must say, Lem! I don't see why you can't take
him along on that hike. He just rushed upstairs and

slammed the door of his room, and it absolutely breaks my heart—I can hear him in there and— Why *can't* you take him?"

"Because he's too little, hon."

"He's just as tall as Patty Vogt, if he is only— I'll bet he *weighs* just as much, too!"

"Can't help that. Downey's not a Scout. When he's twelve years old I hope he'll be a Scout. Vida, it wouldn't be fair to the other boys in town."

"But he loves to go to the woods, and he wouldn't be any trouble at all! You're only going as far as the railroad cut and—"

"Just because I'm Scoutmaster I'm not going to offer pleasures to my son which other kids can't have. Probably there are a hundred nine- and ten- and eleven-year-olders in town who would like to go on a Scout hike, and if they can't go—and they can't—I'm not going to let Downey go."

"He's crying as if his heart would break—"

Something turned over inside Lem's chest. If there was anything he couldn't stand, it was to see Downey cry. Thank the Lord, he almost never did cry. "It won't break, Vida," he said stoutly.

Later on they got Cub Scout activities started in Hickory, and this problem was reduced. But that

was after Downey's time. Downey entered the troop with the midwinter herd of Tenderfeet, five weeks past his twelfth birthday.

Repeat after me the following: "On my honor—"

Second-Class in the spring of '29, First Class that fall. Then came the merit badges, then came Life and Star. Downey broke his leg when he was fifteen and that slowed him up on the Eagle Scout business. He didn't get to be an Eagle until he was sixteen, in the spring of 1933. Later, in response to a unanimous invitation from the Scout Council, Downey Siddons served as an Assistant Scoutmaster until he went away to college.

His broken leg. It healed perfectly, but it took a long time. It happened down at The Spires, a series of rocky cliffs on the river, where they went for their summer camp.

"Everybody must understand this. Get it straight, guys. There's to be no mountaineering, no climbing on The Spires!"

"Aw," came the moan of disappointment.

"Sorry, but that's the law. I just talked to the farmer over on the next place, and he tells me that a girl from Fort Dodge was killed here last year, trying to climb out on that tallest pinnacle. The sandstone's mighty crumbly, and can't be trusted. Any boy of this Troop who climbs on that sandstone will be sent home. That's that. Dismissed!"

The very next afternoon Lem was across the valley, examining an Indian mound with some boys, when distant laughter and a whistle or two drew his gaze beyond the willows. Far on the sharpest ledge of red sandstone a slim khaki-clad figure was crawling. Grim and determined, Lem headed his amateur archeologists back to camp; they splashed through rocky shallows of the river, and arrived at the tents.

But not before a treacherous knob had dissolved, not before Downey had grasped at roots and bushes and had them tear loose, not before he had ended up in a gully below. Other boys, frightened and pale-faced, were carrying him into camp when Lem got there.

"Your leg's broken. Both bones," Lem said ruefully when he had concluded his examination.

Sweat was thick on Downey's high forehead. "I'm sorry, Dad."

"Patterson and Stover, you take joint charge of camp until I get back. I've got to get my car and take Downey to town and have his leg set. Downey," he exploded, in pain and worry and wrath, "why in the name of—? Why did you deliberately disobey that order and climb on that—? Those Spires? Why?"

The wide clear stare beating against his own. . . . "Dad, I— I don't know. Something just came over me. We were up there—back from the edge—and it looked so—exciting. The ground, far below. Seemed like I just had to see what—what the ground looked like, straight down. Like I was in an airplane. So—"

Lem asked, after they were in the car and skimming over the prairie, "How do you feel?"

"Lousy," came the grating voice from the rear seat. "Just one thing: Dad, it's only the second day of camp. Can't I—come back? After they set my leg? 'Course I can't go on hikes or— But then I wouldn't miss the evening campfires, and everything. And I'd get to watch the athletic meet. Dad, can't I?"

"Remember what I said? Yesterday?"

"But, damn it, Dad! Haven't I been punished enough already? This broken leg ought to remind me." Wrapped in his blankets, Downey seemed poised between anguish and desperate laughter.

"I said any boy who crawled on those rocks would be sent home, didn't I?"

"Yes."

"Downey, let's look at it like this. You imagine you're the Scoutmaster, and you made a rule and stated a penalty. Exactly what would you do, in my place?"

The boy was silent for a solid mile. "I guess," he said, in an unsteady voice, "that I would make me stay home."

"Good. I'm glad you see it that way."

Vida and her mother were visiting relatives in Marshalltown, so Lem had to install Downey in the hospital until camp was ended. . . . Downey himself made the suggestion, pleadingly. No sense in worrying the life out of Vida and spoiling her holiday. Lem and Downey agreed to keep their secret.

"You'll have plenty of time to meditate," said the father.

"I'll say I will," croaked the half-drugged youth. "About rocks and Spires and treacherous sandstone and such. Dad, you'd better get back to camp. It's a long drive. . . ."

"How do you like Creamy Joyce as a bone-setter?"

"Doctor Joyce? He's swell."

"He'll look in on you in the morning. Downey, eighteen years ago Kermit Joyce was—"

"I know. You told me. G'night, Dad. . . ."

Lem stood beside the bed until the boy slept, which wasn't long. Then, instead of driving directly to camp, he went downtown to Pinkie MacPhee's electrical appliance shop. Pinkie worked late at the shop often, and tonight was no exception.

Lem stood among the radios. "Pinkie, which little bedside radio was it, that Downey was so crazy about?"

Pinkie came striding over to the shelves, his braces tinkling, and dug down beneath. "This white one, Lem. It's a darb! He said he was saving money, hoping he could buy it by fall. So I've been sort of holding it out of stock for him."

Money, money. 1932. Ah, the butter and egg business that year. Nobody in Iowa seemed to have any money, any more. "I want it now," said Lem and took out his wallet.

Back to the hospital, the low light, the motionless sleeping body, the heavy snore—probably that was from drugs. A nun stood smiling while Lem arranged the radio by his son's bed.

Downey could draw delightful cartoons; that talent had helped him win his merit badge for Art. He sent a great scroll through the mail—it was

77

Doctor Joyce who mailed it for him—and the R.F.D. man presented it to Lem when he halted at the camp mailbox.

. . . Lem was haranguing attentive Scouts, Downey was sneaking away, he was climbing on the cliff, the stone was crumbling, Downey was falling end over end—thousands of feet, apparently—Downey was landing with a thud. It said, in ornate capitals, *A Scout Is Obedient*. Down at the bottom was Downey in bed, his leg done up in a cast ten feet thick and twenty feet long, listening contentedly to a radio as big as the Farmers National Bank. "There's music in the air—" with notes all over the place. "Thanks a million, Dad."

THANKS *a million, Dad.*

If it were possible to hear pleasanter words than those, Lem Siddons didn't know what the words might be.

He lived, deeply, intently in some portion of each boy's life; he had dwelt with as much humor and wisdom as he could manage, in many hundreds of such hidden portions. But through his son he found a rare completeness. It seemed sometimes that he was walking with Downey's feet; so was he baffled and annoyed by the cruder truths of existence, as Downey was thwarted or enraged.

For Downey Siddons was a miraculous being; you had only to look at Vida's glowing face to see that. Left to herself, Lem imagined that she might have spoiled the daylights out of their child . . . he saw to it that there was no spoiling. With all his soul he could forgive Vida her doting impulses. . . . those years of maidenhood, when other thin-breasted girls said they were going to have two, six, ten children . . . when other girls actually named the vague infants to be born in their best future. Forever, through that ordeal, in Vida rankled the verdict of doctors; ah, it had not been intended that she be fed this bitter pill, but she had found out, she had found out. Why all those intimate examinations, why the X-rays of her broken pelvis, why the specialists? She had learned. Emptiness filled her before in truth there was an emptiness.

So God and obstetricians were gentlemanly and generous. Downey was here, treading the earth, swimming the water, dancing, praying with his mother and father, teasing his grandmother, getting into fights, tumbling into a dozen peculiar kennels of puppy love. There could be no more children, but plenty of women wholly normal in body possessed but one child, and were happy so.

Vida Siddons shone through those years with a

80

luminosity which kept her as a kind of ageless dryad —graceful, womanly, benign or trivial, embracing each dawn with ecstatic arms. Little crinkles of silver came to crease her blowing bobbed hair; she laughed at the silver . . . Lem insisted that she had more freckles, and much prettier ones, than when she was a girl.

Within and without the home, Lem carried his unwieldy burden of boys with the easy fortitude of an old campaigner. Sometimes he made mistakes . . . oh, sure. He was far from perfect, but he admitted to imperfection even to himself, and that was half the battle.

Not every boy who passed khaki-clothed along his life might win the world's respect and the Scout master's pride. Severn Lewis: that was a riddle to stand unsolved. He had been persuaded away from his pool hall haunts by some of the older boys; at fourteen he joined the troop, became First Class, won the annual sliding contest, won the 220-hurdles and the half-mile run at camp, and all within a year. Then suddenly he didn't show up at meeting any more; Sev had five merit badges within his grasp, but neglected to complete the final achievements for any one badge. Some of the boys talked to him; finally Lem had a long talk with him . . . what was wrong? Lem couldn't find out. Sev Lewis wouldn't speak frankly; he hinted that the Scouts bored him, and he'd better drop out. Next year he was arrested for selling obscene books to some schoolboys. Figure it out. Lem couldn't.

Not every boy from the town's alleys became a Creamy Joyce. Creamy had gone into the Navy at seventeen, spent two years on a mine-sweeper—and reading medical books the while, no matter how rough the North Sea weather. He worked his way through the University of Iowa and Johns Hopkins, married the daughter of one of his own professors; he came back to Hickory and took over Doc Hillsen's practice when Doc's health was failing. Alert, keen, resilient, warmhearted: Kermit Joyce was a joy to all.

But—not every boy—

Misfits, fallers-by-the-wayside: yes, there'd been some. Toby Hickling was avoided as the town drunk by the time he was twenty-one. Joe Chattler went to the reformatory at Anamosa for auto theft, and Tip Arrum got a girl into trouble and was forced to marry her, and was arrested for beating her savagely. Ugly records, sordid records. But those were just about the lot.

No, the Boy Scouts of America weren't an infallible remedy or panacea; neither was Lemuel Siddons. But nowadays he could walk the street—

Gus Schemmerhorn, manager of the movie house. A Scout. "Hey, Lem, look at the feature tonight. Our hometown marvel again. They say this is the best one yet." Lem would stop to examine the posters under glass. Seek Me Forever, with Ernest Danton in the leading role. Bones Danton, they had called him, about 1920. His father ran a cleaning and pressing business for a couple of years, there in Hickory. Bones was the best swimmer and diver of that period; three of his camp records still stood.

Paul E. Partridge, Attorney at Law, read the sign hanging across the way; but Paul wasn't in his office just then—no, indeed—he was in the State House of Representatives, down in Des Moines. Scout . . . Bunker & Son, Best Groceries: so they were, the best grocery store in town—independent, better than the chains—and there was Jackie Bunker waving between placards which crowded the long corner windows. . . . Dr. Kermit Joyce, Physician & Surgeon. . . . MacPhee Electric Shop. . . . Morton Katz, Insurance. L. Corral, Photographic Studio. Wint Lansing, youthful editor of the Hickory *Herald*, was just darting across the street with a bundle of mail in his hand. Scout, Scout, Scout.

Far in Chicago, San Francisco, New York, Miami —name the towns, name the names, remember the badges and contests, the awards, the rewards. (Lem Siddons had his reward, every waking moment of his life and in his dreams as well.)

How about the foreign places? There was that Twenty-fifth Anniversary picnic, postponed from winter until the summer of 1939, simply because there wasn't any public dining room in town where they could fit in all the people who wanted to attend. So they held a wiener barbecue and basket picnic out at the State Park, and Lem was presented with an engraved gold Swiss wristwatch which could tell the seconds, minutes, hours, days, months and years and centuries—a watch which could chime, sound an alarm, estimate the speed of moving objects, and do practically everything else but recite the Gettysburg Address.

Five hundred and nineteen cars at the picnic, Sheriff Roy Bixby counted them. (Scout.)

The word had gone around, not just around town, but around the world. A committee sat with lists of names, and the committee sent out letters, months before. So, before the watch was presented to Lem up on a rustic platform before those thousands of people, Postmaster Rudy Dorston—Scout—produced a regular United States mail sack, unlocked it, and let letters and telegrams and cablegrams pour across the table in a flood.

Lt. (j.g.) Harris Pitwell, in Mediterranean waters; Benny Oppenheim, with the United Press in London; Artie Paks, vice-consul in Madrid. Teddy Henderson, with a rubber company in Brazil. Lt. Col. Pres Meadows in Alaska, Jasper Wentworth at the Sorbonne in Paris, Chris Hedge missionarying in India, Dayton French with Shell Oil in Venezuela, Whitey Manchester teaching school in China, Jig Zanias with a shipping firm in Greece, Handy Chilton doing something in Havana—

"I don't know exactly what Handy's doing in Havana," said Lem, over the little loudspeaker which Pinkie MacPhee had set up, "but I'll bet it's got something to do with girls!" The roar went high.

OWNEY had graduated with a Bachelor's degree, but no direct aim or purpose insofar as Lem and Vida could see. Two years at Ames, two at Chicago . . . he had studied electrical engineering, commerce, philosophy and other arts and sciences which did not shape into an integrated whole.

"How about the butter and egg business?" his father suggested roguishly.

"Dad!"

"Well, it's a living."

"*Just*, to the best of my observation. . . . No,

Pappy, it hain't that. I know you never wore no shoes until you was nigh onto man-growed but—"

"Well, what's better than making a living?"

"You know the answer to that one, Dad. Doing something that you want to do, that you're wild about, that you've got a complete yen for! Doing something which occupies all your dreams, awake or asleep. Something you're really het up about."

"Such as?"

"Wish I knew. . . ."

That was the year before. In 1939 Vida and Lem made the day-long drive to Chicago to see their bachelor receive his sheepskin. That night they all had dinner at a famous restaurant, in celebration; just the three of them— Downey had no girl-friend whom he cared enough about to bring along.

They'd expected that he would drive back to Iowa with them, but Downey shook his head. He had some tag-ends to finish up, at the University . . . a loose end or two, things to look after . . . he was very vague about this, but the parents did not press him because he seemed so serene—serene almost to the point of being smug.

"Wonder what that kid's got up his sleeve?" Lem said, as he reached over and turned off the light in their hotel room.

"Search me, darling," came Vida's sleepy voice through the dimness. "But whatever it is, it's good for Downey. He fairly emanates self-satisfaction."

"Think it's a girl? It didn't seem—"

"Decidedly not a girl."

"How do you know?"

"I," said his wife, "am a woman. Or have you forgotten?"

No urging was needed to persuade Downey to be present at the Twenty-fifth Anniversary picnic. To Downey this was a much more important event than his own graduation. A telegram arrived in Hickory, lamenting delay; finally he reached home the morning of the great day, with June sun rich on every tree and lawn. He had sat up all night in a bus in order to save money.

No time for palaver, no time for questions to be put or a confidence to be volunteered. Downey had his shower and shave, squeezed himself into the Assistant Scoutmaster's uniform which was now too tight for him, and away they went to the State Park —to the speeches, the messages, the watch, the tears which blinded Lem when he tried to respond properly—the songs which sounded like hymns under a blissful sky.

It was a Sunday, and no one might say Nay to the Siddonses when they wanted to take a good long nap after they reached home. Of course Lem had been too excited down at the picnic to eat much of anything, and he was ravenous when he woke up. There were smells in the air, enticing smells.

Lem put on his glasses and peeked out of the window. If you please, Downey was just in the act of barbecuing some short ribs of beef on the back-yard charcoal grill. He had the table set, there beside the peony bushes, and on that table there were rolls and milk and fruit and a big crock of potato salad made as only Downey could make it. Lem shut his happy eyes, contemplating the dabs of green pickle, the bits of tan bacon, moon-shaped slices of hard-boiled egg, circlets of pink onion, the pungent yellow of homemade mayonnaise coloring the whole. . . .

"Hurry up and get down here, you two. Want your rolls toasted or just warmed up?"

"Toasted!" screamed Vida from the bathroom.

"Three orders toasted! Coming up—"

They felt that he would talk, this night; talk he did. They were close in the dusk, sphinx moths were busy all around them, a night hawk squawked high above, and Vida put her head in her hands for awhile. But Downey couldn't see her, because by that time it was too dark.

. . . Remember how he was always fooling with toy airplanes when he was a kid? Remember all his boyish interest in aeronautics? Remember how that was the first merit badge he qualified for? . . . Well, yes . . . he had been flying, a little, in Chicago. He'd taken a few lessons—all he could afford. And his philosophy prof had been in the RFC during the war, and he talked a lot when they were having a bull session.

"That's me," said Downey. "Remember the time I nearly broke my neck, down at The Spires, trying to see how the ground would look from the nose of an airplane? Well, that was me, too."

Lem said, "You sound so—sure."

"Dad, I am sure. Mom, don't you start sniffling about dear little Downey winging around in the air, because they'll probably have me on the ground in a lot of mean, nasty, boiling-hot classrooms for a long time to come. It's a little place known as San Antonio, Texas; and I shall be known as a Blue Cadet."

"Oh, darling, it's all over and done? You've actually—enlisted—without telling us?"

"Beautiful, it was something I *had* to do! It came over me, this spring. So—you see— I'm now twenty-two, and didn't need parental permission. Just thought I'd surprise you. And also thought that I wouldn't subject myself to a series of lectures known as, From Bird-man to Angel in Ten Easy Lessons, or, How to Talk Downey Out of It."

Lem kept clearing his throat. "When do you leave?"

"Soon as my orders come through, or so they tell me. I have been accepted as a candidate who will try eagerly to make the grade as an Aviation Cadet in the United States Army Air Corps. They just dote on husky little college boys like me."

Both of them had thought of his being— Well, what could a soldier do except—kill? Even in the air—

"Exactly that, good people. Slay or be slain. What **is** the world doing this minute except rumble, rumble, rumble? All the philosophy I learned at school was not filtered through the mellifluous accents of the great and good Dr. Guilfoyle. You pick up a lot in bars and cafés and on park benches, and riding on the bus, too. I've heard enough pro-Red or pro-Pink or pro-Hitler or knock-down-and-drag-out-

91

general-anti-American chatter in Chicago to drive me silly."

He stood tall and restless, kicking at something in the darkness. It turned out that he was kicking an overripe peony to pieces. "You never preached at us kids in the Scouts, Dad. Maybe that's one reason why you've been such a howling success. You're more successful right now than any man I know— and at a job which has never paid you one red cent, but which has actually cost you God knows how much money, in the past twenty-five years."

Lem muttered, "Thanks for the orchid, son. This is surely orchid day for me. Guess I'd better start a greenhouse."

"You didn't preach, but you set an example. And in a way, our community set an example too. It has now come over me, in my scrambles through the mystic catacombs of higher education, that we've got the best little working machine on the market. Germany builds a lousy machine, so does Russia, so does Italy, and we don't want to be a farcical wasting-away monarchy like some poor folks we know, or a defunct republic like you-know-who, bled dry and emasculated by wars. But suppose someone else has other plans for us? And do they just! Read the papers, children."

So he orated whimsically, laughing at the world, laughing at himself the while, and with that deadly earnest stream of firm decision running underneath the froth of his slangy jest. All Vida could do, in the end, was to call him over to her for a kiss; and Lem went down to the basement and at last found in an old cupboard the thing he sought—a pair of half-pint angel wings, pink and bedraggled, constructed of cardboard and cheesecloth. One time Vida had made them for some motherless Scout to wear in a minstrel show. Lem brought the wings upstairs and pinned them upon Downey, who was boldly drinking a man-sized beaker of beer in the kitchen.

Vida didn't cry until after they were in bed; Downey never knew that she cried; he may have guessed. Lem lay staring into the dark for a long time.

He was afraid of airplanes. Pesky things—they went so fast and made an awful lot of noise.

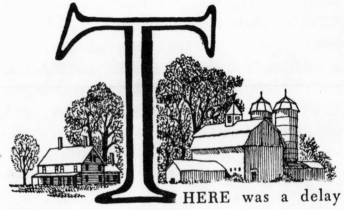

HERE was a delay before Downey reported for training in Texas: some business about filling up the class to which he would be assigned. The Siddonses made the most of their opportunity. They had picnics with friends or just by themselves, every evening when the weather was favorable, and sometimes when it wasn't.

One night they camped out all night, below Millard's Bridge; Doctor and Mrs. Kermit Joyce and their ten-year-old son came along. They lay beside the fire and told ghost stories, and ended up with a mixed sextette singing Negro spirituals with such verve that an old farmer dressed and came down to the woods to see what all the hollering was about. That was the night when proud little Frankie Joyce took a nine-and-a-half pound catfish on his trot-line —a bigger catfish than any of the others had ever caught in their lives.

Stars, stars, the sky between the stars and beyond them. The recollection of a day in nearby Millard's Lane, when a Jeffreys touring car broke down. Fair summer woods still unspoiled, and peopled with hundreds of shades in cotton uniforms or just old overalls, hastening noisily with knapsacks and bundles of lunch. Every grove, every eroded ridge on the hillsides, the big glacial boulder bulking in low-flowing rapids: all could tell their stories of the young feet which had walked that way. The stars. . . .

As was usual, Troop activities slumbered through the summer after camp was done—too many boys had summer jobs, or went away to the lakes with their families. Come September, things would be buzzing again. But there was one chore which must be gotten out of the way, and that was the Sixteenth Annual Local History Contest. Uncle Winton Lansing of the *Herald* inaugurated that in his will, and young Wint now kept up the good work. A prize of twenty dollars, cash, and a small silver medal, to the Scout who wrote the best fifteen-hundred-word paper on some phase of county or town history. Indians, railroads, coach lines, wolves, outlaws (very few) and prairie fires had received vigorous attention during those sixteen years.

"Still got your medal, Downey?"

"But certainly. The twenty bucks—I spent that."

"What was your paper?"

" 'The Murder of John Ross at His Pioneer Mill.' I understand that it reached a record low for Neatness, but my sheer genius of style pulled it through."

"Well, listen, Genius. You've got to help me out. There are three judges—new ones each year, as you will recall—and I've got a good two dozen entries to be judged. Aunt Lottie Crosley, from the library, will be one judge. You will serve as Number Two—"

"O.K. Who's the third?"

"There's been a new English teacher in high school this year and everybody says she's smart as tacks. Name's Gress or something like that. Yes, that's it—Janet Gress. She stayed on to teach in the Junior College summer school. Mind stopping in there on your way home this afternoon, and asking her if she'd object to being a judge in our contest?

She won't know much about local history, but at least she can judge from a literary standpoint."

Afterward—well, not too soon afterward—Downey told how it happened. The building had been remodeled since last he was inside it, and corridors were changed. He was told to stop at Room 217, on the second floor: that was where Miss Gress could be found. He searched in vain for 217 (mistake in the office; the woman behind the desk should have said 207) and was on the point of going back to the office for help when a little gypsy of a girl came dancing up the stairs.

She was a flurry of tucked peasant skirt and gaudy blouse, she had a bright scarf tied over her black curls, she looked to be about sixteen at first glance. "Honey," said the lordly Downey Siddons, from the height of maturity and sophistication, "will you please tell me where I can find Miss Gress?"

"Right in here," said the sprite, and darted ahead of him into an empty classroom. He entered to find her seating herself behind the desk, with much billowing of her skirts and jangles of her bangles. "I am Miss Gress," she said. "And what can I do for you, you great big grown-up man, you?"

She was ten months older than Downey.

They had their first date that night, they were together every evening—and some noons, for lunch
—until Downey went to Texas. The Sunday before
Downey departed, all the Siddonses drove with
Janet to a farm near Clarion which was her birth-
place and her home. Her father was a drawling red-
faced giant who was modestly well off because of
the meat-carrying proclivities of Hereford cattle and
Duroc hogs.

Herman Gress's obsession, to Lem's delight, was
the collecting of such ancient artifacts as could be
found in gravel pits or plowed fields; he had three
cupboards on the long back porch crowded with
these relics, all scrubbed and shiny and quite im-
properly labeled.

Tiny little Anna Gress—about four-feet-nine, like
her daughter—owned the most beautiful collection
of patchwork quilts that Vida had ever seen any
time, any place.

The match was made in Heaven, the love was
consummated in Texas one day after Lieutenant
John Downey Siddons got his pilot's wings, in 1940.
. . . Janet and Downey were living in Hawaii, and
Janet was a few weeks away from her confinement,
on December 7th, 1941. Downey was one lucky
pilot who managed to get off the ground and tangle

98

with the Japanese that day. His parents and parents-in-law were inordinately proud of this.

He finished the war in command of a fighter-squadron covering the B-29's of the 20th Air Force; Janet did not have to plead long and hard with him to desert the fly-business, which he did as a lieutenant-colonel. Downey announced that he was heartily sick of airplanes, as who else shouldn't be, and that he had been offered a swell job in a New York advertising agency by the brother of a former group commander. But Lem noticed that he hung onto his commission in the Reserves.

HEY'D never stressed the religious angle too much in the Scouts. A Scout Is Reverent—sure. For a time Lem Siddons even taught a Sunday School class at church, but that was long ago. He gave it up, to the minister's expressed disappointment, because he felt frankly that he was subtracting a certain thought and energy from his Scout work, and he thought the Scout work was more in his line.

There were cranks in Hickory, just as there were cranks everywhere. The Reverend Mr. Minton Lappsley came around and exerted pressure on

Lem, time after time, until Lem thought that he would dive out of the window. Mr. Lappsley was pastor of a weird sect who squawled and jumped at their services in a dirty frame building near the electric light plant. Mr. Lappsley said that in the Boy Scouts, Almighty God had definitely put a worthwhile instrument into—well, almost pagan hands. No emphasis on Christly activities; no mention of how Jesus would have been a Boy Scout if they had had them in Galilee? . . .

He supplied Prohibition leaflets which he demanded that Lem distribute to the Troop; and in this campaign he was roundly seconded by Mrs. E. Sarah Backerdick, a gaunt creature with protruding eyes and a black mustache. Mrs. Backerdick wanted the boys to go around treading upon every cigarette butt they saw. "Grind them with the heel"—that was her term. She felt that if all the Scouts devoted themselves assiduously to this task, and kept an accurate record, they might grind with the heel as many as one hundred cigarette butts, each, in a single day. That amounted to 36,500 butts per Scout per year.

Lem managed to keep his temper through several sessions with these Great Minds, then finally he exploded. Thus he was the object of contempt in a sermon preached by the Reverend Lappsley, and in a letter which Mrs. Backerdick sent to the *Herald* but which Editor Lansing stormily refused to print. The detractors attempted to set up a rival boys' organization to be known as the Krist-yan Komrades, which died in its incubation.

. . . Also there was Mr. Ivan Apgar, a fulminating atheist, who threatened to withdraw his son from the Troop because the Scouts had repeated the Lord's Prayer in a service at camp.

"It's not all peaches-and-cream," said the exhausted Lem, following his interview with Apgar.

"But *you* are," said the adoring Vida. "The peach in my cream and the cream on my peach!" There was something blissfully therapeutic in Vida's kisses; Lem declared that they made a weary old man into a vibrant young one.

Some Troops had regular Bible reading, but Lem figured that his Scouts could get that at home or at church. In elder years of his life, however, he turned more consistently to the Bible. This Scripture business, of course, dated from the month of March, 1951, when an Air Force C-54 went homing upon a peak in Alaska, and of course everybody aboard went homing with it.

He thought dully, through later months, that

everything would have been much easier if Vida would only talk. That silence, that staring, the often-closed eyes, the close-pressed mouth . . . oh, it was hard to take. Hard, hard, hard.

Janet was living with her children in the State of Washington when it happened. She'd gone there to be near Downey as long as she could, after Col. Siddons was summoned to Active Duty. John, Anna, Vida and Herman: those were the four. Their photographs romped thickly upon the mantel of the Siddons' fireplace.

"What was it that woman was reported to have said, during World War Two?" Lem pondered, as he sat with Vida in the June dusk. It was much the same sort of evening as it had been when Downey told them that he was to be a Blue Cadet . . . how long ago? Twelve years. . . .

"Something about— Oh, I know. 'Wars aren't won by losing other people's children.' Something like that. 'Other people's boys,' I guess it was."

Vida's tight voice said, "That wasn't a war. Read the papers."

"Um. I know. 'Police action.'" Lem lit the candles in the hurricane lamps beside him, and picked up his Bible. "Guess I'll read awhile. Want me to read aloud?"

Vida didn't answer. So often she didn't answer, so often she sat in some lonely dark realm, and Lem couldn't seem to call her back.

He began to read aloud; he read the Ninety-first Psalm all the way through; he'd always appreciated that one, but somehow it was the first verse and the fifteenth and sixteenth verses, which gave him the most satisfaction.

Vida's head was a fluffy knob of silver, the way the candlelight held it. "I don't like that," she said sharply.

"No? How about the Twenty-third?"

She spoke scornfully of David's promises. " 'Snare of the fowler.' It caught Downey, all right. 'Noisome pestilence and terror by night.' What bosh and drivel! Was he able to tread upon the lion and the adder and dragon, and trample them underfoot? No, of course not. They trod on *him*, they trampled *him* . . . oh, Lem, Lem, Lem!"

It was better now, after those several months, because she could cry. At the start she couldn't cry. Not a tear.

"If only he'd been flying that airplane, instead of the pilot who was! He was such a wonderful flier— he might have avoided that crash— But he was

104

just a passenger, going out to his new command. And he had to sit there and take it."

Lem said, "You know, I think he was asleep. Probably most of them were. Never knew what hit them. That's what General Bowman suggested, according to Janet. You know—figuring out their flying time to that position, and everything."

"What matter if he was asleep? The mountain—just reached up for them."

Lem arose and went hunting for a pipe. He'd never smoked much, through his life; but Downey loved to smoke a pipe, and there were several of his old pipes still in the house. Lem enjoyed the glowing of tobacco crumbs, the drift of perfumed smoke. He thought it rested his nerves; and of course the pipe itself built a wonderful bridge between himself and his son, wherever that son might be.

"Way it seems to me— Maybe that mountain reached up for a very special purpose. Somewhere, off in space or—or in some other dimension—there were folks who needed Downey and those others, more than we needed them. That's what I try to tell myself, anyway."

"Not more than Janet and the kids! Not more

than us. Oh, Lemmy, I wish the children were here, now. All of them. I wish Janet would bring them *now*."

"Hold your horses, lady. She's bringing them next month. She would have brought them sooner, if Baby Herman hadn't had that virus and stuff. So—you'll have a wonderful summer with them."

"Oh, yes, driving back and forth to Clarion all the time. You won't catch Anna Gress letting them out of her sight for long!"

"Well, I don't know. Anna's generous. She'll go halves."

She came to kneel by his side and put her arms around his thin knees. Ah, more and more like her old self, at last; it was the tears which had helped . . . he knew it. Now the scalding fluid welled in his own eyes. . . .

"Lem, I've got a notion. Small town living: Downey loved it, and you know how Janet swears that she was always lonely on the farm. Furthermore, if she wanted to live at home, they'd have to build an addition. Well. What about our old house? Ever since Mother passed away I've let the Fishers have it, but we've never talked about a lease. . . . Just for a year or so, anyway, so we can have a real good taste of the children? Lem, let's ask Janet. Let's *plead* with her."

He said, "Sounds good. She might like that. She knows lots of young folks in Hickory; a bunch of those former scholars of hers are married now, and they've got kids just about the same age as—"

He yawned prodigiously. "Wow. I've got to get to bed. Promised to go out and inspect the model campsite where those MacPhee kids are staying, in Watling's Woods. They're both trying to earn their merit badge for Camping. I'll have to drive out early, before I go down to the depot."

She rose with him, and picked up a hurricane light. "Why bother to go down to the depot at all? Mazie and Herb Corral will handle everything, and handle it beautifully. You know what Creamy said to you this spring: 'Take it easy, kiddo.'"

"Well. . . ."

Lem blew out both lamps. He and his wife stood close together in the night. Half a moon hung on the western sky, and miraculously there appeared a streak of thin mercury, boring past the moon—perfectly straight, like metal rising in a glass.

"What on earth's that, Lemmy? A flying saucer?"

"Just a jet plane, hon."

"From the Air Corps?" Vida could never learn to say Air *Force*, though Downey had tried to teach her.

"Probably so." Lem was still thinking of the Ninety-first Psalm. "Don't take so much umbrage, Vida. After all—"

"What—?"

"I mean, that Psalm. We must remember that it's given peace and courage to countless other folks. Maybe even to—to Downey, when he was first flying. And that first verse, and the last—"

In his arms she said, "Quote them, please, if you can."

He took a deep breath. " 'He that dwelleth in the secret place of the most High shall abide under the shadow of the Almighty. . . . With long life will I satisfy him, and shew him my salvation.' "

O HELP other peo-ple at all times; to keep myself physically strong, mentally awake, and morally straight.

Johnny's voice, Downey's voice, the tone of a thousand others.

It wasn't an Open Meeting. They'd just had one in January, and here it was the end of February, and already a new herd of Tenderfeet clamored for admittance. So there was nothing to do but hold another initiation, and bring in all seven of them.

The boys appeared in alphabetical order; there was a Boyce, a Coversen, a Garth, a McDonnell, a Richardson, a Senfadder. Siddons came last of all.

Lem was weary, and all the emotion—

"Raise three fingers of your right hand in the Scout sign, and repeat after me the following: 'On my honor—' "

Johnny's face blurred before him as the oath was repeated. . . . He heard himself saying, "Scout John Downey Siddons, I take great pleasure in presenting you with your Tenderfoot badge!"

The deep voice of one of the older boys bellowed from the back row, "Hey, that's Lem's grandson! How about it, guys?" They rah-rahed for awhile until Lem held up his hands in mock anger.

Over and done, over and done. The other boys gone, Johnny gone, the paper work not done at all, and winter squeezing closer through the empty building. Oh, it was late. He hoped that Vida hadn't awakened, and worried. How long had he spent shuffling in a solitary trance along the walls of that room, looking at the service flags, examining photographs, peering blankly at butterflies and faded moths in their makeshift cases—staring at Abraham Lincoln's picture, and Washington's, and Eisenhower's?

Friday night, February 27th, 1914. That was when it all started, here in this same room. And tonight was Friday, February 26th, 1954. Sometimes forty years didn't seem like forty years at all. Sometimes it seemed like a week . . . sometimes it seemed like more years than were lived by Grandpa Jeremiah Axline, 8th Illinois Volunteer Infantry, who died there in Hickory in 1946—the last old soldier in the county, one hundred and two years old—and nearly the last one in the State of Iowa.

But it would be forty years tomorrow, and not a word had been said. Maybe people were waiting for Lem to conclude fifty years of Scouting before they gave another picnic. Or, more likely, the town and the Scouts had used up all their energy back in 1939, when they offered the barbecue and the letters and telegrams, and the watch.

So he was tired and he was cold—and he was old—and he was going home with a sense of tasks unaccomplished, important deeds never performed.

His ears and his imagination were playing tricks on him . . . shouldn't happen, not when a man was only sixty-four years old. Things like that happened in one's dotage . . . he could hear feet coming up the stairs.

Pinkie MacPhee's leg braces. They jingled and clumped in a peculiar fashion, quite unmistakably.

Always had, even when his crippled legs were aged only by a dozen sad little years, and the braces were smaller. . . .

Pinkie and Creamy Joyce stood before him. Lem grunted; he took off his glasses and rubbed them well. It was a relief to know that this was not mere illusion.

"We saw you burning the midnight oil."

"What are you two highbinders doing up here at this time of night?" he demanded.

"Members of the Scout Council have a perfect right up here at any time," said Doctor Joyce airily. "And well you know it!" He put one skilled, muscular hand behind Lem's head and clamped the other on Lem's chin. "Open your mouth for the doctor, and say, 'Ahhhh.'"

"Ahhh," said Lem. When Creamy released him, he said something else.

"Fine talk for a Scoutmaster!"

"Well, you brought it on yourself, with your high jinks!"

Pinkie MacPhee was examining framed snapshots, as he always did. "Hey, Creamy. Come here . . . 1915 camp. Who's this character directly behind you, in this group in front of the cook-tent?"

Doctor Joyce went to peek and conjecture. "I

112

think that's that kid—Donald? Don Something. Father peddled horse medicine and stuff to the farmers; they lived here only a year or so. . . ."

MacPhee shook his big bald head. "No. I think it's Beany Watson."

Lem came to look. "You're cross-eyed, both of you. That tall fellow is Sid Lovitt and he never came back here after the war, but he wrote to me when you got up that Twenty-fifth Anniversary business. He lives—or did live—in Providence, Rhode Island, and he's in the meat business."

"He always knows," said Creamy. "Guess that settles it."

Lem said, "Come on, I was just on the point of leaving. Who's going to give me a ride home?"

"What did you do—walk down here?"

"Oh, yes. Johnny was up to take supper with us, and he wanted to walk so he could demonstrate how well he knew that antique Scout pace—fifty steps running, fifty steps walking. Recollect that nonsense?" and they all chuckled, remembering.

Lem added huskily, "Johnny's a Scout. He received his pin tonight."

They laughed and shook his hand.

"Now I'm wondering how I'll feel when my *great*-grandchild becomes a Scout," Lem told them.

After silence, Pinkie said, "Doc. Let's get down to brass tacks."

Lem looked at them both, and as soon as Creamy was speaking, the entire hall began to float within Lem Siddons' gaze.

. . . Went up to your house, but you weren't home, and she guessed you'd probably still be here. So we came. . . . No, it was the regular Council Meeting tonight; you know we changed to the last Friday of every month, because too much was going on for some of the members during the first part of each month . . . unanimous decision fully agreed to by the whole Council . . . too much to ask of any man your age, and after all these years . . . you'll probably kick your head off, but it isn't fair to you to let you continue . . . no, no, *no, damn it all,* no one has complained; no one would ever complain, if you lived to be a hundred . . . it's a case of sheer justice and decency and expediency! Expecting a man who's been doing it for forty years, to still get out with a bunch of savages and hike all the way to Tunnel Mill every week. . . .

Voice said, "Creamy. Let me sit down."

Lem sat on the old kitchen chair behind the old kitchen table, and began to cry.

Pinkie said, "You want me to dive down the stair-well, you just keep that up."

In more practical fashion, Doctor Kermit Joyce came around and took Lem's pulse. He shook the watch on his wrist. "You'll live, Lem," he said. "Probably about as long as Grandpa Axline."

"You mean— Give it all up?"

"No, you lunatic! You didn't give us half a chance to finish. No—not give it all up—not until they carry you out to the burning ghat and we all dance around, making whoopee. No, for God's sake! You're to be Scoutmaster Emeritus. Ever hear the title before? Neither did we. We invented it, right here in Hickory. You'll give the benefit of your experience, the benefit of your advice, the lovely gifts of your wisdom, the fund of your laughter, the knowledge-able touch, the sweetness and light and love! You'll attend any meeting you care to attend, any hike, any camp, any campfire. But—and this is from your hoary family doctor—you'll never again have to act the part of a sprightly buck, in those hours when you don't feel like winning the Olympic races."

Lem said presently, "I'm not exactly a hundred and two."

"Who was it," asked Joyce, "who sat by the roadside out White Fox Creek way, fanning himself languidly, while ten Scouts stood around to offer First Aid, and thirty-five others started running wild in the tall timber? And on a cool November day, too? Who? I tell you, Lem, the very trees have eyes and ears."

Lem Siddons said, "Oh, shucks. That was just because I— It was because—"

Pinkie MacPhee relighted his cigar. "I kind of seem to remember a man, long ago, who took a dim view of that Scoutmaster who dropped in from Hawk Center to visit our Troop. The man I remember said privately that such a person was too old to be a Scoutmaster. Not young enough, not close enough to the boys in age; too much of an old man's viewpoint, and so on. That was when you were something like twenty-seven, and the other Scoutmaster was crowding fifty-five."

Lem dried his glasses, put them on, and sat studying the problem, as he had studied so many others, in that room and out of it. "Maybe you folks have got some sense on your side. But there's still the matter of who could take over the main job."

The two younger men nodded at each other above his head.

"Tell him," said Creamy.

116

"No, you'd better be the one."

"I wish you'd both quit talking as if I were a half-witted old scarecrow," said Lem petulantly.

Doctor Joyce put his hands in his pockets. "O.K., kiddo. Lem, who ever hung up a record for merit badges, in this Troop? I think it was nine more than he needed for Eagle Scout, and he was sixteen at the time."

The hall was silent, waiting for Lem's answer . . . might have been that over two thousand ghostly ears waited for the reply.

"That's easy," Lem said. "It was Frankie—your own son. Back about—oh, I'd say the end of World War Two." He looked up at the Council members suddenly, as if half guessing at what was in their minds. "But Frankie's still in Korea. Isn't he?"

Joyce shook his head. "In California, or maybe even on his way back here. He's through, Lem— out of the Marines, or will be very soon. He's going to live right here in town, and George Alexander is urging him to come into the Farmers Bank. If he didn't learn enough in the Scouts, and at college, and in the Marines— If he didn't learn enough to be a good Scoutmaster, then he'll never be a good Scoutmaster!"

"But would he want to tackle it?"

"I talked to him on Long Distance, this afternoon. He's raring to go. But only if you'll remain in the Emeritus capacity."

Lem said in a wet voice, "Guess I'd consider it."

HE NEW Community House wasn't completely furnished yet; Lem had thought that it wasn't furnished at all. It bulked at the corner of Division and Prospect, surrounded by piles of plaster and tiles and scaffoldings; it looked stark and black and unpromising in the staring street lights, and Lem said, "What in the nation are we doing down here?"

But they shepherded him inside and they showed him a room. It was a big room, nearly as large as the old Scout Hall in the school building, and much more conveniently arranged; there was a stone fire-

119

place at one end. Walls were lined with display cabinets; there was a platform where ceremonies or shows could be held; one short corridor led to the Community House washrooms and gymnasium.

"Now, swear on a stack of principal compass points," said Creamy Joyce, "that you'll not let a soul know we ever brought you here. You're supposed to know nothing about this until next week. You see, they've invited the Governor, and he couldn't make it until that date. The banquet will be served in yonder. My own particular job is to select the orchids for Mrs. Lemuel Siddons and Mrs. Downey Siddons. Don't know why in hell the Committee thinks I know anything about orchids!"

High over the fireplace grew an embossed representation of the First Class badge, glaring in gilt against the panels. Beneath that embossing hung something covered with a cloth.

"Want to hold a private unveiling?" asked Pinkie.

"As his physician, I recommend it."

Pinkie found a long pole, and limped to the fireplace. Cautiously he lifted the cloth to reveal a big photograph of Lem Siddons. Lem was wearing a flannel shirt, his battered felt hat was on the back of his head, and his mouth was open and his glasses gleamed, and his eyebrows were on high. Firelight washed his face. . . . It wasn't beautiful but it was real.

Who—? What—? When was that taken? He didn't remember—

"Last summer down at camp," said Pinkie. "Remember one night when Luis Corral and I dropped in on you folks? Luis took it with one of those candid camera gadgets—infra-red or something—while you were telling stories by the fire. I think—" He considered. "You were telling 'The Hound of the Baskervilles.' Boy, how that used to put the fur up on my back!"

"Little bird," said Creamy, "told me that picture was going to be in the Des Moines *Register* next week, and also in the National Scout magazine."

They took him home.

The house was warm, and before Lem turned on the light he could see a red glow from the hearth where a couple of logs were still charring. More than that he saw, a moment after the hall light snapped on. First came a pale hand waving, and then a face moving above the top of the davenport in the living room. He heard somebody muttering, and sort of kicking around. . . .

He went blindly across the half-lit room. *Downey*, he wanted to say, when he saw the tousled hair and

121

sleepy eyes grinning, when he saw the knitted afghan tossed aside, and arms coming up to him.

Lem stumbled over a sheepskin-collared coat which had been tossed heedlessly aside. He thought, *A Scout Is Neat.* Unofficial thirteenth point of the Law. . . .

"Johnny boy. What on earth—? Why aren't you home in bed, down on Division Street? Does your mother—? Does Grandma know you're here—?"

The towhead nodded, violently if sleepily. "I just kind of thought I'd like to visit you tonight, and I asked Mom when I got home, and she said O.K. So I called up Gram, and— So I came."

"You mean— And sleep in your Pop's old room, the way you like to do sometimes?"

Johnny kept nodding. "I like to stay there. All his old pictures and things, and his Scout stuff around on the walls. And that piece of the cast from his busted leg, with the nuns' autographs on it."

"But it's past midnight. You should have been in bed long ago."

"Oh, you know Gram. I guess she's kind of clay in my hands," he added with a giggle. "I asked her— special—because I got my badge tonight, and every- thing. Asked her could I lie on the couch and— And welcome you."

Lem said, when he could speak, "I'm glad you lay on the couch and—welcomed me."

. . . As he crept into bed, Vida stirred and reached her hand toward him.

"Goodness. Thought you were sound asleep, hon."

"Not now. I heard you come in."

"Vida, I— Got something to tell you."

"Is Johnny in bed?"

"Oh, sure. He's got that old plaid bathrobe of Downey's spread out on the foot of his bed, in case he needs it for extra cover. Vida, Creamy Joyce and Pinkie MacPhee came up to the hall tonight and—"

She chuckled dryly, and her hand closed tighter. "You funny thing. Don't tell me anything. I've known, for weeks. They wanted to wait until you gave that badge to Johnny—until it was truly forty years."

After a moment she whispered, "Lem."

"What?"

"It doesn't seem that long. . . . Lem, what's that noise?"

They listened, and perhaps someone else was listening too.

"It's Johnny. Is he talking in his sleep, Lem?"

. . . Could have been a variety of other sounds. Could have been the whistle of a circus train, wailing on the prairie, and far away and with a strange tone; could have been the pounding of young feet on hollow stairs, or the yowling of a pussycat who didn't want to be bandaged, or it could have been a banjo strummed in moonlight or firelight. It might have been the sizzling of ham and eggs in a blackened pan, or the rasping of a "raspberry" snort, or the rattle of wheels on a lumber wagon. Anything in town, it could have been.

. . . Or a whippoorwill whistling its heart out in the musk of early summer, or the gong of an ice-cream sandwich cart, or the popping of an overdone hot dog, or a real live dog scratching at the door and whining to come in. Or a church bell clanging in reminder, or the report of a starter's pistol in a race, or the burbling of doves on a mansard roof, or the clinking of well-earned coins in a pocket.

Or it could have been the crackling of campfire flames, or the cool dripping of water in an artesian spring, or the slam of rifles as they spoke their salute in the graveyard on Memorial Day, or the bird-call of the bugle which followed.

But it was none of these.

"It's Johnny," said Lem Siddons.

"Is he having a bad dream?"

"Oh, no, just chanting before he goes to sleep. You know how kids do."

Vida listened.

"It's the Scout Oath," she said, "I guess he's saying it over and over, so he won't forget."

On my honor, I will do my best to do my duty to God and my Country—

ABOUT THE AUTHOR

MacKinlay Kantor was born in Webster City, Iowa, on February 4, 1904. He was educated in Webster City and Des Moines, Iowa, and in Chicago. At the age of seventeen he became a reporter on a small town daily newspaper, of which his mother was the editor. When the newspaper failed in 1925 he moved to Chicago, working at various jobs connected with newspaper work, and finally, and for the last time, became a reporter again, this time on the Cedar Rapids, Iowa, *Republican*. When this newspaper was suddenly sold in 1927, and he lost his job as a result, MacKinlay Kantor decided that he would devote himself entirely to writing fiction. Since that time he has written twenty-nine books, hundreds of short stories, and many motion pictures. Among his most beloved novels are *Long Remember*, a memorable novel of the Civil War; *The Voice of Bugle Ann* and its sequel, written many years later, *The Daughter of Bugle Ann*—two of the finest dog stories ever written; *Valedictory*, and *Happy Land*, two perfect examples of MacKinlay Kantor's special genius for capturing the full flavor of a small American town. One of the most successful motion pictures of all time, "The Best Years of Our Lives," was based on a long novel in verse, *Glory for Me*, which he wrote in 1945.

Married in 1926 to a young commercial artist he met in Chicago, he is the father of a son and a daughter, and also is a grandfather. Although his home is in Sarasota, Florida, he lived for a time in Spain, where he completed his novel *Andersonville*, which was awarded the Pulitzer Prize in 1956.